MW01153432

Becoming Invisible

Sandy Brannan

Sandra!
This is a
story about a
mother and daughter!
I hope it blesses you!
Happy Reading!
Love, Sandy

To Donna and Cathy, my sisters, who share the same memories
as me

Copyright © 2019 Sandy Brannan
All rights reserved.

ISBN-9781694639042

Chapter One

That closet had not been opened for many years. It wasn't because it contained a big secret; there had just not been time to explore the contents. Time was best spent doing other things, necessary things. There wasn't much that needed to be done anymore though.

Squeaking as it opened, the closet accepted the light from the room revealing the boxes covered with dust on its floor. They looked just like they had decades before, only the dust hinting at the passage of time. Having not been opened in many years, there was so much trapped inside of them. Years before they had simply contained photographs, but they now held precious memories of a lifetime ago.

Ella sneezed as a bit of the dust found its way to her nose. She felt like closing the closet door as soon as she realized the memories she had tucked away for so long were locked tightly in the boxes she was now staring at. She hated to cause herself the pain she knew was to come, but she knew she needed to find some closure soon because, at her age, time was running out. Wiping her nose with the sleeve of her housedress, Ella found herself suddenly feeling a bit tired. Glancing at the window, she noticed the sun had barely risen. She knew the weariness she was feeling had nothing to do with the time of day. Just looking at the boxes, she felt a strong urge to run away. Many times over the last few months she had almost opened that closet door, never quite able to summon the courage to actually follow through.

This time would be different she told herself as she pried the lid from the box of photos. And she actually believed it for a few seconds even as her hand shook with the effort. Then she saw the picture resting on top, the faces of a happy family staring up at her. The tears were falling before her fingers lightly caressed the photo.

She let herself go as she stumbled out of her bedroom toward the couch and the memories.

*

Ella winced as she stood up, one hand still holding the dust rag she had been using all morning while the other went around to the small of her back. Something didn't feel right in her body. If she were to be honest, something had not felt right for the last month or so. Looking around at her clean house, she wished she could call it a day. A nap sounded really good to her about right now. A loud crash from the boys' room brought her back to reality. "It will be years before I can take a nap in the middle of the day," she thought as she rushed down the hall to see what her three young boys were up to now.

"Momma, it wasn't me, I promise!" Ella wasn't even sure which one of her boys said it this time.

"Y'all clean up in here, and be in the kitchen for lunch in ten minutes," Ella responded as soon as she realized there was no blood or broken bones.

Having three young boys was tough. Maybe that was why she was feeling so sore and tired lately. As soon as she thought this, Ella realized the boys had not been acting any more like little boys this past month. No, something was wrong with her. But who had time to worry about yourself when you had a young family to care for? Ella pasted a smile on her face as she entered her kitchen to make sandwiches for herself and her boys.

Later that night, when Frank came home, he smiled at her over his forkful of beef stew, and she felt her worries melt away. Frank had always been able to make her feel better. Smiling back at him, Ella silently thanked God for her happy life. She truly was blessed, and she wondered if she wasn't blowing all this out of proportion.

The next morning Ella struggled to get out of bed. She threw the heavy quilt off of her as she willed her legs to swing out of the bed she shared with Frank while noticing his side was feeling a bit chilly. She could already hear Frank and the boys in the kitchen. Throwing a housecoat on, she shoved her feet into house shoes as she sheepishly made her way toward the source of all the noise.

Frank kissed her gently on her cheek as he whispered, "Hey there, Sleepyhead." into her ear. Ella felt the blood rush to her cheeks, feeling a little bit ashamed of herself. What self-respecting mother slept in later than her husband and children? The boys, all three of them, just stared at their momma. Noticing the bowls of corn flakes on the table only added to her guilt. She usually made a big breakfast of bacon and pancakes before her children got out of their beds. What in the world was wrong with her?

Frank pushed her down into a chair while he offered her a cup of coffee. "Would you like some corn flakes? It was the best I could make." Glancing down at the cup of coffee, Ella whispered, " No. Thank you though." as she felt her stomach do a funny little flip. Somehow the thought of corn flakes floating in a bowl of milk made her feel sick. The more she dwelled on that thought, the more the feeling became a reality. Pushing away from the table as she covered her mouth with her hand, Ella rushed to the bathroom to throw up.

When she came out, Frank had sent the boys outside. "Honey, what's going on with you? Are you sick?"

Ella thought a minute before she answered him, "Not sick, not really anyway. I don't know how to explain it. I just don't feel like myself. I wouldn't be worried except that it's been like this for about a month." Looking up in time to see a quick flash of anger in her husband's eyes, Ella wished she had told him before now. "I thought it would just go away, and I really didn't want to worry you."

"Well, I am worried. And you're going to the doctor. Go get dressed right now."

Ella didn't want to go, but she also didn't want to disobey her husband. He loved her, and she knew deep down that she did need to go to the doctor. She couldn't fight the small jolt of fear that shot through her at the thought of visiting one though. They certainly couldn't afford it, but it was more than that. Doctors scared her. She knew it was irrational, but she couldn't shake the feeling that he might have bad news for her. But she really didn't have a choice, so she went to her closet and picked out a clean skirt and top to wear to the clinic.

Ella climbed into their car as she listened to Frank explain to the boys to be good while they were home alone. He drove her to town in silence. When they pulled up to the door of the clinic, he sat there without cutting the car off. "Ella, you understand I can't go in there, right?"

She knew what her husband was feeling. He loved her so much that he couldn't bear the thought of hearing bad news come out of a doctor's mouth about her. She just smiled at Frank as she picked her pocketbook off the floorboard of the car. "I'll be right out."

Opening the door of the clinic, Ella noticed it felt heavier than most doors. Shaking her head at her wild imagination, she turned her attention to the doctor's secretary, quickly explaining what had happened that morning and why she was there. The secretary told her to come on back to an exam room to wait for the doctor.

Ella was lost in thought about her three boys when she heard a soft knock on the door. Pushing aside the dark thoughts about who would take care of her children if something was really wrong with her, Ella softly said, "Come on in."

Extending his hand, the doctor smiled as he said, "My name is Dr. Hayes. What's going on with you today?"

His kind manner put Ella at ease right away, and she blurted out, "Something's not quite right with me. For about a month, I've just been so tired and sore all over too. And I've been throwing up most mornings even though I haven't eaten anything yet."

As soon as Ella voiced her concerns, a thought occurred to her. Looking into the eyes of the doctor, she knew he was thinking the same thing too. "Mrs. Wells, do you think you could be pregnant?"

Ella felt the color drain from her face as she felt the doctor gently press her back on the table. "We don't want you passing out now, do we? Besides, I need to do a quick exam if that's okay with you."

A few minutes later, after they had talked a bit more while he examined her, Ella was sure she had her answer. "We could run some tests, but I don't see the need to do so. If everything you have told me is correct, I think you and your husband will have a new baby in May. Do you have any questions for me?"

Ella couldn't think of a single question to ask the man. Ten years ago, another doctor much like this one had told her that she would never have another baby. And she hadn't, so why now, a decade later, would she suddenly be pregnant? None of it made any sense to her.

"Mrs. Wells, are you sure you're okay? I can stay and talk to you if it will make you feel better. "

"No, no, I'm just surprised is all. I'm fine, really. Thank you so much, Dr. Hayes."

After the doctor left, giving her one last smile over his shoulder, Ella slowly lowered her body from the exam table. Entering the small closet-like room to remove the gown the nurse had given her to wear, Ella stumbled. Reaching out to steady herself with one hand against the wall, Ella placed her other hand over the small of her stomach. Looking at her semi-flat stomach in the mirror on the wall, Ella considered that it wouldn't be flat for much longer. Still struggling to comprehend that she was carrying a baby inside of her, Ella quickly dressed as she considered how to tell Frank.

Ella couldn't help but notice the way the nurse smiled at her on her way out of the office. Surely she wasn't the oldest mother-to-be the nurse had seen before. What would her boys think? Ella's mind was swimming when she opened the car door and glanced up into the anxious face of her husband. "I think I'm fine, but the doctor said he could run some tests. Let's just go home, okay?"

Frank nodded as he put the car into gear, still as silent as he was on the drive over. They were both lost in their own thoughts as Frank pulled the car under their carport. Ella jumped out, and went straight to their bedroom to change out of her skirt and top. Deciding the best thing to do was to cook supper like she did every night, Ella went to the kitchen and took out the lard, flour, and buttermilk to make biscuits before she started the chicken. Cooking supper was something Ella could do without thinking, which was a good thing right now since her mind was not on the chicken she was about to fry. She always felt a little bad when she made this meal for her family. She had to chuckle as she remembered the first time one of her boys had made the connection between the chickens that pecked around in their yard and the delicious platter of fried meat on their table. Joe had been about five years old at the time, and had asked about his pet chicken as he was grabbing a leg off of the platter to put on his plate. Ella had not expected Frank's quick reply. "Well, buddy, you're about to eat your chicken's leg right now." Joe had dropped the food quickly, looking to his mother for an explanation. So she told him that they raised their own food, adding that was how God had designed the world. Once Joe had it explained to him, he had eaten his supper, although he didn't ask for a second piece like he normally did. Ella continued to laugh as she thought about how all three of her boys had come to the same realization over the years. Thinking of her boys when they were young caused Ella to touch her stomach protectively. Would this sweet baby think their chickens were pets too? She simply could not believe she was about to experience becoming a mother of a newborn again. It still had not quite sunk in.

"Come on, it's time to eat," she hollered from the kitchen about an hour later. During that time, she had decided to just tell her family all at the same time. Laughing as her boys stumbled over each over as they found seats around the family's small table, Ella sat down too. Frank looked at her with one eyebrow raised. She knew this was because she rarely sat down to eat with them, preferring to make sure her boys all had eaten before she gave herself any food.

Ella waited until her family had finished eating before bringing up her doctor's appointment. Frank shot her a quick look, telling her without words that he knew she had lied to him earlier, but his irritation was instantly replace with concern as he waited for Ella to share her news. Noticing how all three of her sons had stopped eating as they stared at her made her determined to get her news out as fast as she could. Facing the worried faces that were staring at her from around her dinner table, Ella spoke quickly. "Well, the doctor told me I have nothing to worry about. But I am going to get a lot fatter, and we'll soon have to pull the old high chair and crib out of the shed."

Frank almost knocked over his chair as he rushed across the room to pull Ella into a hug. "Oh, I was so scared. Thank God you got good news." He kissed her softly as he whispered in her ear. As he pulled back from her, she couldn't help but marvel at the tears welling in his eyes. Slapping her sons on the back as he made his way back to his seat, Frank told the family, "This is the best news we have had in a long time."

The boys seemed to take their cues from their daddy as they all rushed over to hug their momma too. Ella just soaked it all in, smiling over the heads of her boys at her husband. Frank gave her a shrug and a sheepish grin as he winked at her. At that moment, she realized he had wanted a miracle as much as she always had; she saw in his eyes the same desire for a little girl that she was feeling in her own heart. "He wants a girl as much as I do," she thought as she smiled back at him.

The boys started talking at once, obviously excited about the possibility of a new baby brother. They started throwing around names for a baby boy, quickly arguing over which name was best. Ella shooed them all away so she could clean up the dinner dishes in peace, secretly happy her boys didn't seem the least bit jealous about the new baby.

As Ella listened to her boys' chatter shift from baby names to a game they had created long ago which involved the unlikely mix of cowboys and toy soldiers, she gave herself a few minutes to think about the tiny baby within her before she gave herself over to the sink filled with dirty dishes. She wanted to pinch herself as she thought about her daily life, and how she had really thought she was living a dream come true. In the back of her mind, she often felt a twinge of regret that she and Frank had never had the little girl they dreamed of. But she had always known this was not her decision. Only God made decisions like that. But now it would seem she was going to have her dream come true after all.

Drying the final fork, Ella wondered briefly if they would be able to afford a new baby. Then she realized how quickly her thoughts had moved from God to herself. She knew she could not handle the added burden of a new baby, but she also knew God would never give them more than they could handle. She worked hard, as they all did. And she knew she had been blessed to find ways to spoil the family she felt blessed to call her own. She knew everything would be all right. Ella hung the dish rags up to dry as she left the kitchen in search of Frank. She needed to feel his arms around her, needed to hear him say again how happy he was about their baby.

As the days turned into weeks and months, Ella's trim figure started to spread. Since it had been almost a decade since she had delivered a baby, Ella found herself thinking back often to all three of her births. She still wanted to pinch herself. When the doctor told her ten years ago that she would never give birth again, a dream had died within her. Did she dare hope that her growing belly was hiding that dream? Oh, how she wanted a little girl. She and Frank had not spoken of it, but she found him looking at her with a faraway look in his eyes, and she knew he wanted a girl as much as she did. She also knew he was remembering their first pregnancy, and how she had nearly lost their oldest child. With that baby weighing in at over a dozen pounds, when it came time to give birth her body just did not quite know what to do. At 21 years old, Ella certainly did not know what to do either. What she did do was pray, and then scream, through the pain and the blood she felt rushing from her body. By some miracle she could only attribute to God, her son finally came out. Perhaps he heard the doctor threatening to cut him up and remove him in pieces and decided to come out on his own. Either way, Ella shuddered as she remembered the serious discussion the doctor had with Frank that day in May of 1928. He asked Frank which one he should save. He said the only hope of saving Ella was to cut the baby up. Frank never answered the doctor; he turned pale as a sheet as he grabbed Ella's hand and told her to please try harder. They were never the same after that day. As much as he had always loved her, that day was when they had truly become one.

The time finally came for their new baby to be born. By the end of nine months, everyone in the family had claimed this baby as their own. Even Joe, already a teenager, was quick to run into the room when his momma yelled out that the baby was kicking up a storm. "Oh, let me feel!" he would say every time as his momma took his hand to position it exactly over the sweet baby kicks she knew she would be feeling for the last time with this pregnancy. Although the doctor had not told her to expect this one to be her last, Ella knew this baby was a gift, more so than her first three. She had decided to thoroughly enjoy every minute of her pregnancy, and she had so far. Jimmy and Timothy were usually too busy playing outside to understand the opportunity they were giving up by not placing their hands on their momma's stomach. But every time they did feel their new baby kick, they would smile at each other instead of engaging in their usual sparring. This new baby was already bringing the entire family closer together.

Ella had been up since dawn shelling butterbeans on the front porch. Even though it was only mid-May, it was already a scorcher.

As she sat in the metal chair with a bowl of beans and shells in her lap, she let the breeze lift her housedress up a little in an attempt to cool off. When she finally could not stand it anymore, she stood up to go find a cup of cool water from the kitchen. As she stood, she felt warmth run down her legs, and she knew it was her time. Thankful that it was still early, she went inside where Frank sat reading his Bible verses for the day. Smiling that smile she always saved just for him, Ella said, "I think our little girl is on her way." His head snapped up as he said, "It's a girl? How do you know it's a girl?" Feeling a little ashamed all of a sudden for getting his hopes up, she told him, "It's a feeling I've had since that day in the doctor's office. I just know this is our last chance, and I believe God is gonna bless us with the desire of our hearts. Now come on! I need to get to the hospital unless you want to help deliver this baby at home like you did the other three." Remembering what had happened each time with the birth of their boys, Frank was more than happy to help his wife get ready for the trip to town.

As Frank helped Ella walk into the hospital, they heard a nurse softly singing a song to herself. They listened to enough to know the words would always remind them of today. Frank looked at Ella, mouthing the words of the song to her in an attempt to put a smile on her face. Grimacing, she attempted to smile back at him, but she simply hurt too much. He reluctantly relinquished her to the nurse who had appeared by Ella's side with a wheelchair. He knew his place was in the waiting room, so he found his way to a seat to nervously await word of his wife and their newest child.

Pushing through the pain, Ella felt every one of her 34 years as she labored to help her baby leave the safety of her body and enter the world. She didn't quite know what to expect since this was the first time she had given birth in a hospital, but some things are the same no matter where you are at, and Ella quickly remembered the pain. She also knew relief would be coming soon, and she was beyond grateful that she had the kind of doctor who would allow her to remain conscious during the birth of her child. Having attended plenty of home births, he did not see the need for the use of drugs that so many of his colleagues were now relying on to assist women through what he considered to be a natural event for them.

The doctor instructed Ella to rest a minute before getting ready to push yet again. "I think this time we might get to see your baby's head." And the baby did not disappoint the doctor as her momma pushed hard enough to allow the doctor to see the head full of hair emerge. "One more push and your baby will be born." was all Ella needed to hear. Scrunching up her face until it turned red, she pushed with all her might, ready to see her precious child. "You are my sunshine, my only sunshine..." echoed in Ella's mind as she felt her baby wiggle free of her, and into the hands of the smiling doctor. When he told her she had a new baby girl, Ella's first thought was of Frank. "I can't wait to tell him," she thought as she drifted off to sleep.

Hours later, when Frank was allowed to see her, his first words to her were "We have a Sugar Doll. Our very own Sunshine." And their new baby was pure as sunshine to them with her black-as-ink hair and beautiful hazel-gray eyes. Ella knew another girl had found her way into her husband's heart as she watched Frank hold their baby as if he thought he could break her. She could not have been happier to move over and make room. Realizing this baby was truly a gift from above, they decided to name her Catherine Grace.

*

Ella wiped tears from her wrinkled face as she laid down that first photograph, smiling through her tears at the memory of her only daughter. Looking at that picture had allowed Ella to return to a time when her house had been filled with the laughter of a family. Memories of pure joy and happiness, long before anything had threatened to destroy them. Placing the lid on the box of photographs, Ella decided to go take a nap before she tackled more of her clean-up project. At 80 years old, she had learned long ago to pace herself. She knew how much of the story was left. She could only hope some of the memories stirred up from the photograph did not enter her dreams. She desperately wanted to remember only the good times before she had to face the nightmare that had invaded her life so many years ago.

Chapter Two

Ella woke up from her nap but did not see the need to immediately get out of bed and back to her task. One good thing about living alone was that she did not feel the need to do things any certain way. She had long ago stopped eating at predetermined times, and her sleep patterns soon followed suit. Now Ella simply listened to her body, letting it guide her. The days were gone where she would find herself at the end of a long day of hard work, wondering how she had gotten there as well as what she had to show for all her effort. Lately Ella had learned that the clock was not her friend. She tried not to look at its face too often.

But she did still like to stay busy. Being busy kept her mind from wandering too far. Ella had learned many years ago to keep her mind under control. And now she had to laugh at herself. Her current task of cleaning out old closets had caused her to do the one thing she had kept under control for many years; her mind was wandering its way back to a time she had buried long ago. But Ella also felt a sense of urgency, almost as if time would run out if she did not tackle this project now. She did not dwell on the feeling too long. She did, however, decide to stick to her plan, and she knew she could not do that while still resting.

Swinging her legs over the side of the bed, Ella grabbed the dresser with one hand to steady herself, knowing she could not afford the luxury of a fall. Who would hear her if she cried out in pain? She waited a few seconds to make sure she was not going to become dizzy before she stood up. She mumbled to herself that growing old was not for the weak as she slipped her worn house shoes on her feet. Shuffling to the closet, she took a deep breath. Confident that she was finally ready for what was inside, she opened the door and reached down for the next photograph. She simply picked up the one her hand landed on. Upon seeing it, she wished she were back in bed, this time with the covers pulled up over her face. She was not sure she was ready to go back in time to where this picture wanted to take her.

But she had been raised to finish what she started, so she made her way back to the couch to spend some time with her memories. Settling back against the crocheted pillows that had been on her couch for several decades, Ella looked at the picture in her hand. Smiling, even though her heart was breaking just a little, she closed her eyes as she went back in her mind to when she was a much younger woman. Determined to not allow too much sadness in at once, she thought back to when Catherine was still a baby. Ella was not quite ready to go exactly where this next picture wanted to take her.

*

After spending a few days at the hospital, Catherine came home wrapped in a soft pink blanket, and carried in her momma's arms, quickly filling the house with the soft mewing sounds of a newborn baby. The boys were in awe, dropping everything to pick her up whenever she cried. She never had the chance to have a truly wet diaper, or to cry for any length of time. Between her parents and her three brothers, she was almost always in someone's arms. No one ever mentioned spoiling her. She was their girl, plain and simple, and they would all protect her no matter the cost.

"Joe, put Baby Catherine down. She can lay there on her pallet for a minute while you come and help me." Joe reluctantly listened to his momma, and gently made the baby comfortable on the thick pallet made of quilts Ella had sewn together with her own mother many years ago. Ella sighed as she quickly realized Joe could not focus on his chore because he kept glancing back at Catherine. "Oh, go pick her up already!" Hearing his momma's words, Joe gave her a quick kiss on the cheek as he ran to pick up his sister. Ella soon learned this was the way it was going to be with her four men. They adored Catherine, and held her as much as they could. Knowing this brought a secret smile to Ella's heart. She was more than happy to do more chores if it meant her boys were spending their time loving on her sweet baby girl. After all, she often spent hours just holding her little baby when the rest of the family was busy somewhere else.

Ella looked down at Catherine before snuggling up to her. When Catherine's little hand grasped one of her fingers, Ella felt a tear fall from her eye. "Dear God, is this how my momma felt when she held me? I never knew until now." Now the tears really flowed as this thought made Ella understand her own mother in a way she never had before. She wondered why these truths seemed to always be discovered when it was too late.

Catherine was weaned before Ella realized what had happened. She was no longer content to let her mother hold her. She saw her older brothers playing, and thought she was as old as they were. They snuck her food from their plates even when Ella tried to get her to eat mashed-up baby food she carefully prepared for her. Ella had to laugh when Joe put a pickle in Catherine's mouth one night at the supper table. Her reaction scared her brother. Her little mouth spit out the pickle, and then her pout appeared before a loud cry erupted from her mouth. Joe looked from Catherine to Ella as his face turned white. "I'm so sorry. I didn't know she wouldn't like it." Ella just laughed as she scooped her baby up. She knew it wouldn't be long before Catherine would learn to eat everything on the table just like the rest of the family. "No harm done, Joe. She'll be fine. Stop your worrying now."

And Catherine did grow, and her brothers did too. Joe learned to drive, and he often let Jimmy and Timothy tag along with him. It wasn't long before Catherine was begging to go everywhere they went. When she toddled out to the car with her chubby arms lifted in the air, one of the boys would scoop her up and take her into the car for a joy ride. As they drove off, Ella watched from the kitchen window, thanking God for this gentle side of her boys. She was used to them fighting and roughhousing, but since Catherine had been born she had definitely seen a new side of all of them. They were smitten, plain and simple.

One day, when Catherine was around four years old, Frank could tell she wasn't happy. "What's wrong with my Sugar Doll today?"

Tears formed in Catherine's eyes when she heard her daddy ask her what was wrong. Frank nearly lost it; he never could bear to see Catherine cry. "I don't have anyone to play dolls with me."

Frank left Catherine in the family room, and hollered at the boys to come in there right this minute. All three boys ran into the room perplexed by their daddy's outburst. He was not the type to yell at anyone. "You boys go on in there and play with your sister as long as she wants you to. And I don't want to hear one word about what she wants to play. Make those tears go away!"

Joe groaned when he saw the baby dolls and tiny clothes, but he smiled and asked Catherine to go get the baby a bottle so he could feed her some milk. Smiling, Catherine ran to find the baby's bottle, and returned with more baby clothes and a little pink hairbrush too. Timothy brushed the doll's hair while Jimmy asked Catherine which outfit the baby should wear. Ella just stood in the doorway watching, and wishing there was some way she could record this memory. The family did not own a camera, and there was no way to get one to the house right then. However, she knew it would be forever etched on her heart.

*

Ella finally looked at the second photograph she had pulled from the box. It was time to leave the innocence of Catherine's early years behind. She knew her journey could not just focus on the good times, and she needed to remember her daughter as a teenager even though it would bring her more pain than happiness. So she drifted back in time again, letting her memories take her back many decades.

*

Ella and Frank had felt as though God had given them an extension of time. When their three boys had grown and flown, neither one felt the sting of it because of their Catherine. Even though she had grown from a child to a teenager, they still thought she was their sunshine. But they weren't blind, and they had their suspicions once in a while that Catherine was running with the wrong crowd. There had been nights when she had come home from an outing with her girlfriends wearing too much red lipstick. And there were other times that they had questioned themselves about how they were raising Catherine, wondering if they were strict enough. Ella knew Frank disciplined more than she did, but she always supported his decisions even though she had a soft spot for her little girl.

Frank whistled while swinging his silver lunchbox on his walk home from his job at the plant. Caught up in his thoughts about Ella's supper, he almost didn't notice the group of giggling girls walking toward him. But then he heard one of their voices, and he knew it was the voice of his youngest child. Looking up with a smile on his face and in his eyes, Frank's gaze landed on Catherine. The smile left his face when he realized she was wearing a pair of shorts. Frank felt the blood drain from his face as his mind took in what he was seeing. He had told her repeatedly to never wear shorts outside of their home, and here she was, in broad daylight, wearing a pair. Walking quickly toward the group, Frank grabbed Catherine's arm and pulled her to the side. Without even thinking it through, he dropped his lunchbox and used his free hand to swat Catherine's backside. While it was not effective as far as a spanking goes, the shock of it certainly got his daughter's attention. Telling her to head straight home, Frank reached down for his lunchbox using the time bent over to compose himself. Seeing the shocked faces of his daughter's closest friends, Frank simply offered them a small smile as he stayed several feet behind his daughter. When they both got home, nothing more was said. But Frank was pretty sure his little girl had learned her lesson, and would never disobey him again. It hurt him to think he had caused her any pain, but he was beginning to wonder if maybe he had been a little less serious about disciplining her as he should have been. He knew she had him wrapped around his finger, and he hoped he had not spoiled her.

Catherine threw herself across her bed. She was crying, but she could not say if the tears were from embarrassment or pain. She suspected the former. It seemed like all the other girls got to do things her parents did not allow. She knew she had the oldest parents of any of her friends, and she couldn't help but wonder if that was why they had such ridiculous rules. And did all parents lurk around outside the bedrooms of their kids? Many times she and her friends had been sitting on her bed, giggling about boys, only to look up and see either her mom or dad standing in the doorway watching them. That always made the girls sober up quickly.

Ella and Frank knew their daughter often clammed up around them, especially when she had her girlfriends over for a visit. But they assumed this was just the way of young girls. After all, it was the late 1950s, and times had certainly changed since they were both teenagers. She listened to loud music that just didn't make sense to Ella and Frank. As they listened to their daughter singing along about a thrill on Blueberry Hill, all they could do was shake their heads. It just did not make a bit of sense to them. But she was a good girl, and they had liked music too when they had been younger, so they did not deny her this one pleasure. They just knew they would never like the music their daughter seemed to love so much.

A hard worker, Catherine saved every penny to be able to walk to the nearby store for a bottle of Pepsi and a bag of peanuts to pour into it. While this was certainly a special treat since the family was still quite poor, both her parents knew what she really wanted, more than the Pepsi and peanuts, was to see other people her own age. And they suspected the tiny store was a local hangout for teenagers. Even though they both thought this was an innocent way for their daughter to spend her time, Ella especially felt the need to warn her daughter about boys. Since the Air Force base was so close to the store, Ella reminded Catherine every time she went there to not talk to any servicemen. She was confident her daughter would obey her, so she felt like a warning was all she needed to give. She knew Catherine had a different life than most of her girlfriends. Living alone with her older parents had to be a bit boring at times, so Ella and Frank were perhaps more willing than most to give her a bit of freedom. Or perhaps they had started spoiling her the day the doctor told Ella she was pregnant.

Even though they worried a little about their daughter, life was good for Frank and Ella. They enjoyed watching their sons with their new lives from a distance. They were filled with pride as they watched how each of their boys treated their wives. Joe and Jimmy had given them grandchildren, but they were still waiting on Timothy to give them one. They did not have their hopes up for that however. They had both seen, and ignored, the way Timothy's wife looked at other men. Deep in Ella's heart, she knew heartache was coming for her youngest son, but she would never dream of saying anything to him. It was just not her way.

They also enjoyed the solitude in their home when Catherine was out with friends, and relished the sounds of girlish laughter when she was at home. Lately they had noticed she was quieter than usual, bringing fewer friends around to see them. This did not raise any real concerns for Ella. She remembered her life as a young woman and how fickle she herself had been at times.

Maybe that is why when Ella heard Catherine ask her to come into the kitchen she did not notice the quiver in her daughter's voice at first. Maybe that is why she did not think there was any significance to the way Catherine said, "Mother and Daddy, there's something I need to tell you." Hadn't she said these words many times before? But Ella finally looked her daughter in the eye, and that's when she felt her stomach fall. There was a deep sadness there, and a distance, that Ella had never seen before. Her daughter was almost 20 years old, and Ella felt like she was looking into the eyes of a stranger. How could that be?

There was no time for Ella to think because Catherine apparently had just enough courage to spit out what was bothering her. As she opened her mouth to address her parents again, Catherine felt the tears slowly leaving her eyes and trailing down her face. She knew her tears would be her Daddy's undoing. He never had been able to see her cry. Asking both of her parents to sit down, Catherine too pulled out a chair at their small kitchen table. She reached out her hands to touch them even though she was finding it hard to actually look either of them in the eye.

"Mother, Daddy, I have some news for you. It's going to be hard for you to hear, and even harder for me to say. I love you both so much, and I never wanted to let you down. Daddy, I know I'm your Sugar Doll, and it's so hard to tell you what I have to say."

By this point, Frank and Ella were near tears as well. But they were also unable to speak. They simply stared at her as Catherine took a deep breath and continued. "These past few months I have been seeing a boy. A man, really. I knew you wouldn't approve, so I didn't tell you about him. I was sneaking out to meet him, and I'm truly sorry about that. I know it was wrong, and I hope you can forgive me."

Ella was relieved. When she first heard the words "boy" and "man" she was momentarily afraid their sweet little girl was pregnant. She gave herself an internal talking-to. Catherine would never ever have done something that could have made her pregnant. As soon as Ella opened her mouth to say something like this to her daughter, her world came crashing down. "Mother, Daddy, I'm pregnant."

Frank looked from Catherine to Ella and back to Catherine again. He was speechless, and then he was furious. "Who is this boy? Why isn't he here with you telling us this news? Did he force himself on you? Where is he? I have a good mind to go find him and drag him back here to face me."

"Mother, Daddy, he'll be here soon. I asked him to stay away until I told you. We love each other, and we're going to get married. It will be okay. You'll see. He's in the military, so he'll always provide a good home for me and the baby. I was hoping to get married here, in our house. Would that be okay?"

Even as their hearts were breaking, they knew they could never deny Catherine what she wanted. They would meet this boy, and accept him as one of their own. They would do whatever they could to make Catherine's life easier. If that meant taking care of a new baby, then they would find room in their home, and their heart, for the baby of their baby if that's what she wanted.

While Catherine and her parents were still staring at each other not really knowing how to start a new conversation, there was a light knock at the door. Frank quickly got up to answer it, and Catherine and Ella both felt a tremor of fear. What if Frank was not handling this news as well as he appeared to be? He had always had such a mild manner, but this might be the news to push him over the edge. This boy, Catherine had not even told them his name yet, might not see the first punch coming, but would he then raise his fists to the future grandfather of his child?

Frank opened the door, and a young man entered the room. He was clean-cut looking even if he was wearing a leather jacket. It was 1959, and this young man looked like he had stepped off the cover of a movie magazine. It was as if James Dean himself had walked into their humble kitchen. Ella immediately understood the attraction her daughter felt for this man, but she still could not let herself think too hard about what he had done to make her sweet daughter pregnant. No mother ever wants to think such things about her child.

"Hello folks. My name is Anthony Williams. I love your daughter, and want to marry her. Today isn't too soon for me!"

Frank and Ella found themselves speechless for the second time that night. They wanted to dislike this young man. They actually wanted to hate him, but they just couldn't. He was pleasant, and he looked at their daughter like she was the most precious, fragile thing in his world. Frank found himself shaking Anthony's hand, then hugging his daughter around her neck. As she whispered, "Oh, Daddy, thank you!" Catherine knew everything would be okay. She had been so afraid of losing someone, either her parents or the man she loved. She was grateful no one had made her make such an agonizing choice.

Ella watched as her daughter moved away from her and Frank to stand closer to Anthony. She did not miss the smile that passed between the two of them, or the look of relief that crossed her daughter's face. She felt alone all of a sudden, almost like an outsider in her own home. Ella wondered if Frank could feel it too.

They got married that weekend. It had been a whirlwind week trying to find Catherine a suitable dress as well as making all the other arrangements. Ella had called each of her sons to tell them

Becoming Invisible

the bittersweet news. Joe had yelled and cursed when he first heard the news. He apologized to his momma, but Ella silently agreed with every word her oldest son had said. The other two boys calmly listened to her, but she had no doubt they were just as mad as Joe had been at the news. She suspected the three of them would like some time alone with her future son-in-law, and she wasn't sure if she would look the other way if it came to that.

But in the end, Catherine's brothers all came with their families to her wedding. It was obvious to everyone that the boys were not as quick to accept Anthony as their parents had been, but that was to be expected. They were protective of their baby sister, almost to the point of violence. And they were not so forgiving of this man, and how he had violated their little girl. But the marriage ceremony was civil with her brothers doing their best to be pleasant for their girl's sake. Each of her brothers had kissed and hugged her, knowing this would help Catherine feel better about herself even while they each struggled with their own feelings.

Ella found herself weeping softly into her handkerchief as her dreams of watching her only daughter walk down a church aisle to be married by a minister went drifting away. There was no long dress with a matching veil, no flowers, and no friends to witness the occasion. Ella was grateful she had found time to make a small wedding cake for her daughter. This made the day easier somehow, knowing she had been able to contribute something to her daughter's happiness. It wasn't enough though. She had always dreamed of her daughter's wedding day, and none of her dreams had looked like this day. In the end, it was a short wedding, with the simplest of vows spoken, followed by a slice of cake to be enjoyed by all. And then it was all over.

Little did Ella know, but this wedding was the first of many dreams she had for her daughter that would die a premature death. As she watched the newlyweds drive away in Anthony's car, Ella knew her life would never be the same. Ella did not miss the fact that her daughter never looked back, never smiled at her parents, or gave them her usual quick wave. No, their daughter was staring straight ahead in that car. She was looking to her future, with the man she loved, leaving her life with her parents as a diminishing image barely visible in the rearview mirror. Her daughter would come home as a visitor now. She would never again live under the same roof as her parents. Ella and Frank really only had each other for the rest of their lives. They were back where they had started, but somehow they had lost control of the very life they had created. It was an unsettling feeling, and Ella had to wonder if Frank was feeling it too.

Looking up at her husband as they told their sons and their families good-bye, Ella wondered if every mother felt this alone when she no longer had a child living at home. She wanted desperately to know how Frank felt, but she knew she would never ask.

The two never spoke of it. Such was the way of married couples during that time. They put the one picture taken at the wedding in a frame to display in their living room as they went on with their lives the best they could. But Ella would often catch Frank just staring at the picture. She wanted to ask him what he was thinking, feeling, hoping for their daughter, but she kept silent. Always the silence. She felt as though a part of her had been removed and thrown aside. Instead of healing, she felt the openness of the invisible wound. No one knew it existed, so no one asked how she was doing. For the first time in her life, Ella felt alone, even though Frank came faithfully home to her every night.

*

Ella looked at the yellowed picture, the frame having been thrown away and forgotten many years ago. She gazed into the smiling face of her daughter. For the first time, she noticed how Catherine had one hand on her shoulder and the other hand on Frank's, as if she were staking a claim. Ella realized Anthony was not in the picture. She thought it strange how he was not in the only picture taken at his own wedding, and how strange it was that she had never noticed until now.

Chapter Three

Ella walked around her house unwilling to look at any more pictures. The wound she thought had closed over years before was gaping. And the rawness hurt. She thought it impossible to feel more pain than she had as a much younger woman watching her daughter drive away from her, but the feeling now was almost unbearable. It had all happened so fast back in 1959. She and Frank had barely had time to adjust to the fact that their daughter was no longer innocent before she was swept away. And once she had a husband, they no longer felt as though they had the right to question her choices. Of course, now Ella knew Anthony as a son more than a son-in-law, but she had to admit it had taken time for her to feel this way. Back then, she and Frank had simply been frustrated by all of it.

*

What did they know about this man? What did they know about their daughter's future? Nothing. All they knew was they had a child living at home with them one day, and by the weekend she was gone, a married woman, left to find her own way in the world. And they were left with an empty quiet house. At times the silence was deafening.

As the months slipped by, Ella and Frank rarely saw their Catherine. Although they remembered being a newly married couple and how they too had wanted to be alone, they still longed to see their little girl. They knew she was busy setting up a new house, and getting to know her new husband, so they weren't exactly surprised that she stayed at her own home most of the time. When she did come over, it was obvious that things could never be the same. As a married woman, Catherine simply was not the same girl she had been to them a few months ago. She was now suddenly a grown woman.

The three of them almost spoke as strangers, especially when Anthony was around. He seemed to be a hard-working young man, and Frank was glad Anthony's government salary allowed him to provide a clean home for Catherine in a safe neighborhood. Frank asked him one day about his job, and Anthony told him a lot of details about airplanes when what Frank really wanted to know was more about his salary and benefits. But those were things one man simply did not ask another man, even if that man had taken his daughter from him. Frank had to resign himself to listening more than talking when his daughter brought her new husband to the house. He always hugged her neck, whispering softly into her ear that she was still his Sugar Doll. Sometimes, when she did not respond, he wondered if he had said it softer than he thought. Frank did not allow himself to dwell on that for too long.

It was what was not said by both Catherine and Anthony that bothered Frank and Ella most of all. Their daughter and her new husband did not talk about the future. There weren't even many conversations about the baby, although that was the one conversation Ella dreamed of having with her daughter. She wanted to know how her daughter was feeling, and if she was scared. She wanted to talk about baby names, and whether there were any family names the young couple might be considering for their soon-to-be son or daughter. She wanted to share her wisdom as a mother with her daughter, to prepare her for the day she would bring home her very own baby from the hospital as well as what would actually happen during the birth. She knew she had never shared these basic facts of life with Catherine. Honestly, she had never felt the need, thinking there would be plenty of time to have such a talk with her one day in the future. Ella had actually never thought about what it would be like when Catherine became a mother, but now that it was thrust upon her, she found herself excited and wanting to spend hours discussing childbirth, caring for an infant, and the ways Catherine's life would change. But Catherine never brought these subjects up, so Ella remained quiet too.

Even though it played a huge role in their future, the young couple also did not discuss Anthony's career in the military with

Frank and Ella. He loved talking about his day-to-day duties on the base though, and how he got to work on the planes. He could talk about this for hours. It was obvious Anthony truly enjoyed being a mechanic. But, even after listening to Anthony go on and on, Frank never could quite get a handle on what the future held for his daughter and son-in-law. He was not naïve enough to think his daughter would live close by forever. He also knew his wife had yet to figure that part out. As country people, they had never lived outside their county, and they never would. All three of their boys lived a short drive away, and everyone knew they would never move away. Catherine had made a bigger choice than even she probably knew by falling in love with a man who had no local ties. Frank could only pray that he would be enough when Ella realized she was truly losing her baby girl. He hoped that day would not come for a long, long time.

The time finally came for Catherine to give birth. She called her parents before she left for the hospital. She assured them she would be fine, and told them to just wait at the house for a phone call from

Anthony. Ella nearly lost her mind when Catherine told her this, but she never let it show. She calmly told her that would be fine, and that they would be praying for her. Her hands were shaking slightly as she hung up the phone and looked Frank in the eyes as she told him what their daughter had just said. Instead of responding, he simply left the room for a few minutes before returning to sit quietly with his wife on the couch.

As they waited at home that night, looking at the phone every few minutes, Ella felt another chunk of herself being torn away. She wondered how many pieces of her heart she could afford to lose. She thought back to a few short months ago when her daughter was living under her roof. Back to a time when she only had to open the bedroom door to sneak a peek at her baby girl. She often had stood there in the doorway just to watch her daughter sleeping, often using that time to thank God for this unexpected gift He had given them all. Now, in the lonely house she shared with Frank, Ella was left to imagine what her daughter was going through. She fought to keep her emotions under control, and she prayed like she never had before.

Ella knew her daughter was in the same hospital where she had been born two decades ago, going through the same pain her own momma had gone through to bring her into this world. No matter how Ella tried to convince herself that Anthony was enough, she knew deep in her heart that her little girl needed her. But she also knew her hands were tied. She was not welcome at the hospital. She did not fully understand why, but she knew she had to grant her daughter this one wish. As the hours ticked away, Ella briefly wondered if she should just show up at the hospital anyway, but something kept her from asking Frank his opinion. Everything had changed in their lives, and her relationship with her daughter was one of the biggest and most confusing changes.

When the phone rang the next morning, Ella answered before the first ring was finished. Anthony laughed and said, "You must have been sitting on the phone." Ella did not bother telling him that she had indeed been sitting beside that phone, wide awake, since her daughter first called to tell her she was on her way to give birth. She did not bother telling him, as Catherine's mother, it would have been impossible to fall asleep knowing her baby was out there in pain. She resisted the sudden urge to scream at him that Catherine was hers first, and would always be hers. Instead she calmly answered, "Anthony? Any news on Catherine and the baby?"

When they learned that their daughter had given birth to a healthy little girl, Frank and Ella wept. They hugged one another tightly, and Ella felt at that moment that maybe Frank would understand if she finally broke down and told him how alone she felt. And she almost got her nerve up to actually tell him, but then the moment passed. Plans were made to go to the hospital to check on their daughter and meet their new granddaughter. Ella knew a new chapter was opening in her life, as well as the life of her daughter. What she didn't know yet was how many changes were coming their way.

*

Drifting back to that time in her life decades earlier made Ella want to dig through the boxes of photos and pull out the ones of her sweet Patricia Marie. She always thought Catherine had the best choice of names when it came to her babies. She wondered now if she had ever told her that. There were so many words that had gone unsaid. Ella wondered if her daughter had ever fully grasped how proud she was of her. If only she could go back in time as easily as she pulled out memories from a box of old pictures.

Chapter Four

The next morning Ella opened her eyes long before the sun rose. She knew why she was awake. There had been no sound to wake her or dream to stir her from her slumber. She knew she would soon be looking at pictures; remembering the joy her little granddaughter had brought into their lives, Ella felt no trepidation about her day. Climbing out of bed, she was tempted to not even brush her teeth or eat her breakfast. But she knew better. She had not survived this long without taking care of her basic needs, so she went about her normal morning even though she knew her time with her photos would be limited today. Jimmy and his wife, the only living children she could claim as her own, would be coming by with lunch and some groceries later. Ella was grateful to Nancy for treating her like her own mother, and she, of course, always looked forward to a visit with her son.

Soon after her breakfast dishes were drying on the small mat beside the sink, Ella made her way to the closet. She thought about a different closet, one that had been full of Catherine's clothes before Anthony took her away. She remembered how many times she had opened it just to stare at the empty rod where her daughter's clothes had hung. She never told Frank she did this, and she doubted he ever suspected a thing. He probably never wondered why it had taken her so many months to turn Catherine's old room into something else. Ella had never wanted that sewing room, but she couldn't just waste the space. She always seemed to sink into a bit of depression when she spent much time in there. The memories were just too strong for her. Shaking the thoughts of Catherine's old room from her mind, Ella turned back to her task at hand. She had pictures to look at, ones that had caused her to wake up in a happy mood. Looking at the pictures today would be different as she planned to dig through until she found sweet reminders of her Patricia Marie.

Just as she suspected, opening the box this morning did not bring any sadness. Ella had determined in her heart to only remember the good today. There was plenty of time for the pain later. She somehow felt she had earned this reprieve from the deep dark sadness that so often permeated her very existence. She planned to enjoy every minute of it. And what better way than by looking at pictures of the dark-haired girl who had stolen her heart so many years ago.

It did not take long to find a stack of yellowed pictures tied together with a faded pink ribbon. Oh, how the memories flooded over her. Making her way once again to the old couch, she smiled as she gave the ribbon a gentle tug, letting the many pictures fall into her lap. She picked them up, one at a time, and determined to let the happy memories sweep her away to better times.

Looking at the pictures of the baby with curly dark hair and an infectious smile made Ella think back to her life as this precious child's grandmother. It was true that Patricia Marie was not her first grandchild, but she was the first one from her only daughter. Somehow that made a difference. As much as she loved her boys and their wives, it was not the same. She had to be on guard around them somehow. With her daughter, she had felt she could be herself. She always assumed the strong bond between daughter and mother could never be broken. As a young grandmother, she just had not found out the ugly truth yet. She found herself enjoying more than just her new grandchild; she was loving watching her little girl take care of her very own baby. It made Ella smile to think of how special it had been to watch her own sweet daughter become a mother. She could not help but remember a time when Catherine took care of her baby dolls as her own mother watched from her spot at the kitchen sink. And now her little girl had a real live baby doll at home to care for.

*

Patricia Marie was crying yet again, and Catherine was just not sure what to do. She had always been the baby of the family, and

Anthony certainly was no help. In fact, he was often not even at home. Catherine knew he had an important job, but she also knew jobs had a quitting time. She suspected he was out with the guys again. But that was not the type of thing you confronted your husband about. Should she tell her mother? She decided that her mother needed to always think things were perfect between her and her husband. So far Mother and Daddy loved Anthony, but Catherine did not want to take any chances. Talking about her husband to her mother seemed disloyal to Anthony, and Catherine loved him too much to do anything that might threaten their love for each other.

But she simply had to talk to her mother about the baby. There had to be a way for her to get some sleep. And maybe her mother could help her understand why Patricia would not stop crying. Yes, she decided she just had to call her mother now. "Hello?" came the familiar voice of an angel over the line. "Mother, it's Catherine. I need you."

Oh, how Ella loved hearing the cry for help, even though she was not pleased that her daughter sounded near tears. "Talk to me, Catherine. Explain to me what's going on, and I'll try my best to help you."

As they talked, Catherine felt herself calming down. "Mom, I have this great schedule written out, but nothing is working out like I had planned. Even though Patricia is only supposed to eat every four hours, she usually cries a lot in between feedings. I just feel bad when I hold her and let her cry until it is time for her next bottle."

Ella replied, "Oh, honey. Feed your baby when she's hungry. Babies don't understand schedules. And there's no good reason for you to have to let her cry just because of the time on some clock."

"Oh Mother I wish I could, but I have been reading this book about babies since before Patricia was born. Dr. Spock seems to really know what he's talking about..."

Before Catherine could finish, her mother cut in, " I assume this Dr. Spock is a man, and I never knew a man to raise a baby. Listen to me, sweetheart. I raised four children without ever reading a single book. And all four of you turned out pretty great. Trust me, and trust yourself. God gave you the instincts of a mother. You know when to feed your sweet baby, so just do it. Don't let some book make you feel like you're not a good mother because you are. And, don't forget, all babies cry. Some cry a lot more than others, and it sounds like our sweet baby girl has a lot to tell us right now."

Wiping her limp hair back from her face with her hand, Catherine had to laugh a little at the way her mother made it all sound so easy, but deep down she felt relieved. She finally felt like everything would be okay. Noticing how quiet the house had suddenly become, she announced that the baby was finally sleeping soundly. "Oh Mother, thank you so much. You made me feel better by just talking to me. I'm just so glad you're my mother. I love you so much." Saying a quick good-bye, she hung up then, promising her mother that she too would go take a nap while the baby did.

When Ella hung up the phone, Frank gave her a knowing look. "You love being needed, don't you?"

"I don't know what you mean." came Ella's quick reply, but she did. She needed to be needed by Catherine. She had felt the loss of her only daughter leaving the house so suddenly, and somehow the birth of the baby felt like a second chance. Hearing Catherine speak words of love sent waves of affirmation through Ella. She wondered briefly if her tired daughter would ever know how happy that one phone call made her.

And it seemed like it was the start of a second chance for them. The ladies became quick friends, bonding over the baby who was growing up as the two of them were growing closer. One thing they did not talk about much was Anthony. He was the reason they were separated, and neither one chose to bring that up. Ella felt certain her daughter loved her young husband, but she simply did not want to talk about him too much. Ella felt deep in her heart that if she ever lost her daughter it would be because of Anthony, and losing her daughter would be her undoing.

Catherine called one day to tell her mother that Patricia had taken her first steps. She had other news soon after that. "Mother, tell Daddy that Patricia is going to be a big sister." Both grandparents were thrilled. They knew Anthony really wanted a boy, so they prayed this second baby would be a brother. They also worried about their daughter giving birth again. Sure, times had changed since 1928 when Ella first had a child, but they both knew there would always be risks with childbirth. And they knew money had been tight for the young family since Patricia had been born. Trying not to borrow trouble, Ella was careful to always be positive when she talked to her daughter about her pregnancy and the new baby it would bring into their lives.

As the months went by, Ella helped Catherine with Patricia as often as she could. She watched as her daughter built a little nest for the new baby. As mother and daughter washed new diapers and knitted blankets, they talked about how two babies would be a lot more work than one. "More work?" exclaimed Catherine. "Patricia sometimes seems like more than I can handle. Oh Mother, what if I am not strong enough for two babies?"

Ella smiled at her daughter and told her, "You'll be as strong as you need to be. It's the way it is with women. And don't expect any help from your husband. You are in charge of these babies. Keep them close to your heart. These years will be a memory before you know it." Then she reminded her daughter of how far she had come. "Do you remember when you tried to only feed Patricia every four hours because some book had told you that was the best way to raise a child? And now look at you; you're a natural with her. She is one blessed girl to have you as her momma."

Catherine wondered about that long after her mother had left that day. Yes, she knew she was a better mother now than she had been in those early first days, but even now the days were so very long, and sometimes seemed impossibly hard. She knew adding another baby was going to make life more than twice as busy. She simply could not imagine a day when there weren't wet diapers waiting to be washed. Every night when her head hit the pillow she was truly exhausted. She wondered if she would ever have a day when she wasn't boiling bottles or trying to find a way to get to the store without asking someone for help.

Time moved on like it does for everyone, and soon Catherine called Ella to tell her she and Anthony needed her so they could go have the new baby. Since they didn't have as much money now, Catherine and Anthony had chosen to have the baby in a clinic instead of at the hospital. This worried Ella, but she supposed it was better than her daughter giving birth at home. Ella spent the night with Patricia that night. She settled her sweet granddaughter into her little bed before making herself as comfortable as possible on the young family's lumpy couch. She would not dream of sleeping in the bed her daughter shared with her husband no matter how uncomfortable the couch was.

The next morning she had barely been in Catherine's kitchen long enough to fix some eggs and toast for Patricia's breakfast when Anthony called to say they had another little girl. Sarah Dianne entered the world almost two years to the day after her sister first appeared. Catherine called her a birthday present since she went into labor on her birthday and gave birth the following day. Ella had

once again waited at home while Catherine gave birth away from

her, but she had not felt the need to sit beside the phone this time.

Watching Patricia had made it a bit easier on Ella, knowing her

daughter needed her to be there for her first child. Ella still missed

being at the clinic, but she knew this was a special moment for

Catherine and Anthony. She could barely wait for Frank to come

over so they could take Patricia to meet the new baby. And Ella

knew in her heart she would not feel completely calm again until

she looked directly into her daughter's eyes to see if she was truly

well.

That night Ella stayed with Anthony and Patricia so he could get

a good night's sleep, even though she hated the fact that her

daughter was alone with Baby Sarah. The next morning, they took

Patricia with them to the clinic to see her momma and her new

baby sister. Ella heard a baby crying as soon as Anthony held open

the clinic door for her. She was shocked when a nurse approached

them saying she was glad they were here because the baby had cried all night. Anthony was furious and Catherine was overwhelmed with guilt when they found out the nurses had left their baby in the hall all night, alone and crying. Catherine wept as she told her mother and her husband how she had assumed the nurses were taking care of Sarah so she could get some much-needed rest. Ella watched as Catherine held Sarah, comforting her in the way only a mother can.

As much as the young new parents had looked forward to a little boy, they were happy with their newest addition to their family. They considered their family complete now because the doctor had given both of them a firm warning to not have any more children. What he failed to make clear to either of them was how to guarantee that did not happen again.

Ella was there when Anthony brought Catherine and the baby home from the hospital. She stayed and helped with the two babies for the next week, often silently laughing as she saw the look of exhaustion on her daughter's face. Ella was not being cruel; she simply very clearly remembered being the same young mother herself. She remembered feeling frazzled, and so exhausted. She also remembered how quickly the days had turned into years. And she was painfully aware of how quiet her own house had become with just her and Frank to occupy the space. She had never fully realized how quickly her children would grow up, and away. She knew there was no way to make her daughter understand any of this. There were things every mother had to learn on her own, so Ella continued to keep her thoughts to herself. She made new memories for herself too. As she stood beside her daughter while they both attempted to dress the wiggling infant, Ella knew she was making a memory she would hold forever in her heart. Even though Catherine was flustered when Patricia pulled at her pants causing her to almost fall, Ella knew she was witnessing her daughter in her finest role. She seemed born to be a momma, and Ella again thanked God for the unexpected gift of Patricia and for safely bringing Sarah into their lives. She smiled as she thought of Catherine one day watching one of her own little girls becoming a mother. She hoped she would live to see it.

*

Ella tied the pink ribbon around the pictures of Patricia, and left the couch to go search in the closet for the packet tied with a yellow ribbon. She had not planned to look at the pictures of Catherine's second daughter today, but the memories of Sarah were stirred up inside of her and she just could not resist. She knew the stack with the yellow ribbon belonged to Sarah. As she found the pictures, she had to smile at the child with the huge grin looking up at her. This baby had always been special to her. She unwound the ribbon, letting the memories come.

*

Ella almost tripped carrying the hot pan of biscuits to the dining room table. She looked down to see which of her impish granddaughters was the guilty party this time. It was Sarah. She had the sweetest grin on her face as she looked up and said, "Sorry Mama, but Patricia made me do it." Ella just grinned. She had heard that one before. Wasn't it just yesterday Timothy had told her the same thing about Jimmy? Sometimes she had to remind herself

71

her own children were grown, and these precious ones did not fully belong to her. But the biscuits had not spilled, and she had not fallen, so she just put the pan down on the pot holder as she bent over to scoop up her sweet little girl. She covered her granddaughter's face with loud kisses, listening to the squeals and giggles that only come from a toddler. She simply could not imagine hearing a sweeter sound this side of Heaven. Oh, how she loved these two girls. And she loved her life. She just couldn't imagine being happier. Things were working out, and she was starting to feel settled somehow about Catherine's life.

Looking up after she gently put Sarah back on the floor, Ella caught her daughter staring at her. She knew exactly what was going through Catherine's head at that moment. She was taking a mental picture, one she would file away to pull out many times over the years. Hadn't she often done that herself as a young mother? She knew that watching her mother love on one of her babies was pure magic for Catherine. She remembered seeing the same look on her own precious mother's face many years ago. It startled Ella a little to realize how quickly she had assumed this new role.

Yes, Catherine knew her mother loved her, had always known. But she was now seeing that love clearly etched on her face. Knowing how deeply she loved her granddaughters touched Catherine in a way she couldn't express, so she just gave her mother a soft smile. As usual, Ella did not need to hear words from her daughter. She knew her better than Catherine would ever understand. She always saw past the falseness, deep into the little girl's heart that still resided inside of her. Ella would always understand Catherine; they were wired together and always would be. No one, or nothing, could separate them.

Stepping away from the moment she was sharing silently with her daughter, Ella approached her two granddaughters again, asking which one wanted the first biscuit. When both girls yelled, "Me! Me!" at the same time, Ella surprised them by picking up a biscuit in each hand. Laughing at their grandmother's trick, the girls watched as Ella dropped a biscuit on each of their plates. They

wasted no time grabbing their treat to put close to their lips.
Munching loudly on the biscuits while they continued to smile at
her, Ella thought she had the sweetest two girls in the world looking
at her. She couldn't imagine being happier. She knew Catherine was
watching her spoil her two daughters. And she knew her daughter
was grateful she was the kind of grandmother who knew her job
was to love and spoil as much and as often as possible.

*

Finding the picture of Catherine with her two daughters brought
Ella crashing back into her day. She sat there quietly looking at the
hands holding the picture. There were so many wrinkles, and they
looked like the hands of an old lady. Who did they belong to? She
softly sighed as she realized she truly was an old lady now. She had
already lived past the number of years she had been promised in
the Bible. She had already outlived so many of her family members,
even three of her own children. But she did not feel the truth of that
right now. Looking at the picture of her daughter and two of her
babies, Ella felt young again. And she felt the youth of her daughter

seeping through the picture too, staring into her eyes. How mature Catherine had pretended to be. How in control she had wanted to appear. But she was young, and she needed her mother even if she was usually too stubborn to ask. This made Ella chuckle lightly as she remembered how she too had once been a self-assured young mother bent on proving her worth. She just wished she had talked to her daughter more instead of keeping so much hidden inside.

"Catherine, Catherine. Why didn't I take every opportunity to share with you how much I love you?" was Ella's cry as she walked to the bedroom to put the pictures back deep inside the old box, pushing it into the closet. Rising ever-so-gently from the floor, Ella looked around her room. She wondered again, as she had a hundred times before, if this would be the room where she would die. She was at peace with her death, but she still had not found her peace with her life. Thinking back on the photographs, she wondered if she ever would.

Ella knew it was time for Jimmy and Nancy to come by with lunch and groceries. She made sure there were no stray photographs on the couch. She did not feel like she could talk about Catherine today. It had been enough to relive so much through the images staring back at her. She went into the kitchen and waited for her company, planning to enjoy an afternoon with her son and special daughter-in-law. She knew they would laugh together, and then the conversation would turn to those who were no longer in their lives. Nancy would try to talk her into a ride to the cemetery like she always did. And Ella would oblige her. They would remember the good times, and the visit would end happily like it always did. Ella was grateful for the visit; she needed a break from her project and the underlying sadness it was causing her to feel.

Chapter Five

Ella had been lost in thought since before her eyes had even opened that morning. Yesterday's trip down memory lane courtesy of the box of photos had been mostly pleasant. Ella had enjoyed reliving those brief first years of her granddaughters' lives. She now knew how quickly those precious years pass for everyone. She had thought she had known that while she watched Catherine raise her girls, but apparently even she had not realized how short the years could be. As much as she wished she had been aware of it when she was in the moment, Ella had learned a long time ago that going back was not allowed. Once you had made a decision with your time, you lived with it forever. That was a truth she had learned the hard way.

Knowing she was going to be pulled under into the wave of depression that often threatened to overwhelm her if she didn't stop it, Ella swung her legs over the side of her bed. She knew from experience that her bed was not the best place for her to spend her time when she felt the heavy load of melancholy heading her way. So she got up, got dressed, and brushed her teeth. Daily habits that seemed so familiar, while at the same time sometimes seemed so ridiculous. Who was she dressing for? Who cared about her teeth? She certainly never bothered with make-up or perfume any more. Ella could not remember the last time she had a visitor show up unannounced at her door. She supposed at this point in her life no one had high expectations of her, so why bother having any for herself? Even as she thought these thoughts, she realized how unfair she was being. Just yesterday she had spent a lovely afternoon with Jimmy and Nancy. And she knew she only needed to call any of her grandchildren or great-grandchildren and they would come take care of her. She was simply feeling sorry for herself this morning, and that was something she needed to shake off if she wanted to survive, and enjoy, the day.

After a simple, and unusually tasteless, breakfast of oatmeal, Ella headed to the closet and the now-familiar box of photographs. She was remembering those early years of motherhood for Catherine as she looked through the box for the small stack tied with a light blue ribbon. These pictures were the ones of her last grandchild, the child she did not expect to get; no one did. As Ella found the pictures and pulled the blue ribbon until a knot formed, she had to laugh. It was such a sad sound, even to her own ears. Ella realized that knot, which she now worked hard at untangling with her slightly bent fingers, represented the direction their lives took after that sweet last baby had been born. There had been signs leading up to it, if only Ella had been paying close enough attention to notice. But she had been caught up in her day-to-day life, and had not always focused on the right things. She realized she was paying the price for that now.

*

When Frank and Ella learned Catherine was expecting a third child, they were afraid. The doctor had been clear years before that Sarah should be their last baby. But Catherine found herself in the family way again. She told her mother that she was happy, but Ella wondered what else her daughter could have said. She knew the young couple must be afraid. What if the birth of this baby meant the death of its mother? How would Anthony survive life without Catherine? How would he manage a job, and a house full of babies? Ella and Frank were certain they were not the only ones thinking these thoughts. But neither one mentioned their concerns to their daughter and her husband. There was no need to. The baby was a fact, growing a little bit more every day inside of its mother. Now all any of them could do was wait, and hope, for the best. And pray.

Ella still spent time with her daughter, but it had not escaped her attention that the visits were now mostly of the uninvited kind. Ella remembered well how busy life could be with a young family. As a young mother herself, an entire day could go by before Ella had realized she had not taken time to eat or even brush her own teeth. She tried to keep this in mind as days went by without hearing from her daughter. Catherine rarely called her mother needing advice anymore either. It was as if becoming a mother for the second time had erased needs and doubts away for the young mother. She seemed confident in a way Ella had never seen before. While this should have been cause for great joy on the part of Ella, it burrowed away somewhere deep in her mind, causing a sliver of worry to take root. She could not quite put her finger on it, but she felt a shift in their relationship. It was nothing they talked about; in fact Ella wasn't sure if Catherine felt it or not. But Ella did. She felt like she was a little less visible somehow in her daughter's eyes. It was a feeling that haunted her every time they were together, and stayed with her long after they parted. No one would have noticed it by the way they acted, but the mother in Ella knew something was not quite the same between her and her only daughter. She knew it would be futile to talk to Frank about it. She even knew what he would say. "You're over there almost every day. What more do you want?" So Ella kept her thoughts and fears to herself, trying hard to keep them hidden and under control.

As Ella watched Catherine grow larger, she knew the day was rapidly approaching for this baby to be born. She already knew she would be the one responsible for keeping the older girls busy while their parents made their way to the hospital for what would be the birth of another sister or the long-desired brother their parents had been dreaming of. The girls knew their brother would be named Richard Allen which they delighted in telling their grandmother, but evidently they had not heard a little girl name mentioned. Ella was curious, but she never asked her daughter about baby names. She always thought that her daughter would tell her what she wanted her to know. She never wanted to do or say anything that would invade her daughter's privacy, so she chose instead to remain silent on so many issues.

When the phone rang late in the afternoon on the last day of September, Ella knew who was calling. "Mother, it's time. I need you to come look after the girls now. I think this baby wants to come quicker than the other two." Ella was already prepared. All she had to do was find Frank so he could drive her to their daughter's house. They didn't live quite close enough for her to walk, but it wasn't too far away either. He could have her there in less than ten minutes. Ella had days before packed a small bag, knowing she would be spending the night away from home soon; she grabbed it and climbed into the front seat, clutching it tightly in her lap. As Frank chattered away, Ella replayed her brief phone conversation with her daughter. She thought of the words "I need you." over and over as her husband's voice droned on in the background. It felt good to be needed, and it felt even better hearing her daughter admit her need. Ella was not being selfish; she was merely happy that her daughter had used those words. Ella needed to be of use.

Knowing this baby would come any minute, Ella made the decision to not make Patricia and Sarah go to bed that night. She got on the floor and played dolls with the two girls. Then she took them in the kitchen to teach them how to make pancakes. They were eating those pancakes drenched in butter and syrup when Anthony called shortly after midnight and said, "Well, we have another one."

Ella knew he was trying to not let his disappointment show, so she put as much happiness into her voice as she could as she asked, "What did you and Catherine name her?" Ella knew her daughter was doing fine, if not Anthony would have told her. "We decided on Linda Grace. Named her after her momma since we're sure now she'll be the last one." What he didn't say was how they were sure, or how he felt about losing his dream of having a boy. Since the answers to those questions were really none of her business, Ella didn't ask. She figured Catherine would tell her if she wanted her to know.

This time Ella was so busy with the two little girls that she had to wait to meet her newest granddaughter. She knew Frank and Anthony both had to work, so she tried to not let herself feel too disappointed. She desperately wanted to see Catherine though and found herself wishing she had learned to drive sometime along the way. She was glad when the doctor finally said her daughter could bring the new baby home five days after she was born. As Catherine walked through the front door of her home carrying her sweet baby wrapped in a white blanket, the first thing Ella noticed was her blonde hair. This baby did not look like the other two. In fact, anyone could clearly see she looked just like her daddy. And it was easy to tell her momma loved her fiercely. Ella knew it was possible for mothers to have favorites. In fact, she had never tried to hide the fact that Catherine was her favorite. And she clearly saw the signs with her daughter; she loved this baby a bit more than she loved the other two. That was saying a lot as Catherine loved her children with all of her heart.

With the arrival of Linda, Ella spent as much time at her daughter's house as she could. She wanted to be helpful without getting in the young family's way. She tried to give the young parents space, choosing instead to play with the older girls or hold the baby so Catherine could take a much-needed nap. As the baby grew, Ella noticed a growing tension between Catherine and

Anthony. Since she would never have dreamed of asking her daughter about it, she patiently waited to be told what was going on. She soon found out why they seemed to be having trouble getting along. One night she overheard Anthony telling his wife that he did not know when it would be happening, but to start planning and packing because they were going to be sent to a new base. They did not exactly argue, but she knew her daughter well enough to hear the underlying tension in her voice.

Hearing about the upcoming move made Ella feel like someone had ripped out her heart. She had not allowed this possibility to enter her mind, ever. Ella was not ignorant to the ways of the world; she had known, deep inside, that her daughter's marriage to a military man carried the risk of her moving far away. She had just never allowed herself to consider it a real possibility. Now the possibility had become a glaring reality. And Ella was scared and sad and beside herself. But she could not let any of it show. She had to appear calm, for her daughter's sake. So, Ella did what she had become a master at doing. She kept her pain buried deep within, making it invisible to everyone around her. She did not speak of the tears she cried into her pillow at night. She found new ways to help her daughter, even though Catherine asked less and less of her. She found new reasons to visit the young family. She watched Patricia and Sarah playing with their dolls while she sat holding Linda close to her. She wanted to soak up the feeling of holding the baby in her arms. Once they moved, Ella did not know how long it would be before she saw her daughter and her three precious grandbabies again. The thought of them moving away had made her almost sick with worry. Knowing they would not be close enough for her to go visit caused a ripple of fear to start at her head and end in her stomach. The feeling was unlike any Ella had ever felt before. She had a hard time controlling it, feeling like if she gave into it she may never be able to come back from where it wanted to take her.

The day finally came that Anthony and Catherine announced their move to South Carolina to Catherine's parents. Anthony was the first to speak. "Well, it seems like I have been given some new orders. Have either of you ever heard of Fort Sumter? It seems like the Air Force thinks Catherine and I should take our children there for a little bit." Frank and Ella knew Anthony liked to make a joke about serious things, and they tried hard to smile for his benefit, but as they watched their daughter struggling to not cry, Frank and Ella knew it may as well have been a move to the moon. They knew it would be a long time before they saw their daughter and her three children again. It made them sad to think of all the ways the three little girls would grow without them there to watch the changes taking place. Saddest of all was the knowledge they had no control over this decision. So they remained silent. And Ella felt herself slip away even more. The young family left to go home soon after Anthony's announcement. Ella sat stunned on the couch long after they had left. Frank stayed away from her, and she knew better than to let this hurt her feelings. Her husband needed the time to process what he had just heard as much as she did.

A week later, Ella went to her daughter's house to help with the packing. The two women talked about how to best pack the dishes to keep them from breaking. They spent a lot of time keeping the three girls from taking the wrapped items out of the boxes. This should have made Ella laugh, but she had a hard time pretending that much. The distance between her and her daughter seemed to be growing, with Catherine seemingly unaware of it, and Ella helpless to expose it. Instead she was forced to paste on that all-too-familiar smile and act like her world was not falling apart around her.

*

Ella did not want to look at pictures any more. She did not want the memories to take her any further than they already had for the day. She certainly did not want to remember seeing Anthony drive her daughter away in their station wagon while the three little girls waved from the back window. She knew they had been excited to go on a trip, completely unaware of how long it would be before they saw their grandparents again.

She wanted to find a way to not think at all, but that was a skill that was harder to do now that she was no longer busy. She supposed she could turn on the television as a diversion, but it had lost its appeal many years ago. She needed something to think about, something that would stop the tears from coming to her eyes because sometimes she felt like if she started crying, the tears would never stop.

Chapter Six

Ella took a few days off from her project. She did not need to rest, but she needed time to mentally prepare herself for the rest of the story. She knew what was coming, and she did not want to live through it again any more than she had wanted to live through it the first time. She laughed a sad laugh as she realized her foolishness on that day her daughter had left for South Carolina. She knew now she would give anything if that had been the worst of it. Moving to a different state seemed so trivial to Ella now, but at the time she had felt like it was the end of her world.

She knew she needed to pull out the old box again, feeling the need for closure, an end to this pain. She somehow thought looking

at the old pictures might once and for all give her the sense of peace
that she had been searching for over the years.

After a few days of pretending not to be thinking about Catherine
and the girls, Ella finally opened the closet again. Before she
allowed herself to reach into the picture box, she thought back to
what the closet used to hold. She remembered the days of hiding
small toys or candy in this same closet. The girls knew she did it,
and they ran straight to that closet every time Catherine brought
them over for a visit. Ella had not thought about the Barbie dolls
and coloring books for such a long time, but she found herself
longing to see the forgotten toys. She had lost her own sweet tooth
many years ago, but suddenly could taste the sweetness of orange
circus peanuts that she used to buy by the bagful. Ella thought how
funny it was to forget something for so many years, decades even,
only to have the memory crash in with such strength to actually
taste it.

Reaching into the box, Ella pulled out a picture of Catherine and
her girls sitting in front of a Christmas tree. She looked at the photo

and tried to find some clues to tell her where the young family had been living when the picture had been taken. She tried to determine the ages of the girls to help her, but as the years had rolled by she had found it harder to remember exactly how old they had been whenever she saw their likeness in pictures. She thought Linda looked to be about seven or eight, so she determined this was taken while they lived in Wyoming. Then she saw the tiny white puppy in Catherine's arms and knew she was right. Linda had sent her a letter telling her all about their new dog they had named Precious. She loved hearing the stories about how Precious kept the young family entertained. One of her favorites was when Linda wrote to tell how it had snowed a lot, so much so that the front door would barely open. She told her grandmother how they had dropped Precious into the snow so she could do her business, only to be frightened they might never find their puppy again when she disappeared. The story had a happy ending, and the way Linda wrote about it actually made Ella laugh. She could clearly tell how much they all loved their new dog.

She remembered all the letters her youngest grandchild had written to her while living there. Her spelling was often hard to figure out, but Ella had taken such delight in seeing a letter appear in her mailbox in her sweet grandbaby's wobbly handwriting. She never received too many letters, so when she did get one it was a special treat. A letter that she would find herself reading over and over. And Ella had saved every single one of them. Linda had been the most innocent of the three girls, perhaps because she was treated as the baby. In so many ways, Linda reminded Ella of Catherine. She was the child who was not supposed to be born. She was the last of her family. And she was treated like the baby she was. Ella could tell Catherine knew she was treating Linda the same way she had been treated as a young girl. This made Ella happy, validated her parenting somehow, to see how Catherine copied her techniques as a mother with her youngest child.

Ella took a long time examining the picture. Had there been any signs? Was there anything in Catherine's expression that should have alerted her mother to what was to come? Ella saw no more now than she had seen years before when the picture had first been sent to her. She told herself now the same thing she had told herself years ago, no one could have known. And if they had known, would they have done anything differently? If so,what? These were questions that had plagued Ella for years, but the time was long gone for finding any new answers. There was no one left to ask.

*

Catherine looked up from the flash of the camera, and smiled at Anthony as he put it away. She knew the Christmas photo would be wonderful whether she and their three girls had been smiling or not. She knew she had just preserved an important memory; one her children would most likely appreciate many years after she was gone. Catherine wondered where such a macabre thought had come from. She had been having those kinds of thoughts more and more lately. At 32 years old, she was certainly too young to be thinking such thoughts about herself. She had never even thought seriously about the deaths of her own parents. Time seemed to be in a holding pattern for Catherine. Life was good. She and Anthony had carved out a comfortable existence in base housing, making many new friends. And Catherine found herself quite enjoying the hours away from home at her part-time job as a bank teller on base. The children took care of each other when they were not in school, everyone feeling very safe at all times within the gated community of the Air Force base they called home. They had settled into life in Wyoming. It was a huge change in weather from North Carolina, but they had managed to find their way. It was easier on Anthony who had been born and raised in upstate Pennsylvania, but Catherine and the girls quickly learned to love the snow and all the excitement that came with it. They made snow angels and ate snow cream, but they also found their way to school and work once they realized life did not stop for the snow out west like it did down south.

As she picked up the pictures from the store where she had left the film last week to be developed, Catherine knew she needed to send a much overdue letter to her parents soon. Even though, deep in her heart, she knew how much her mother and daddy loved to hear family news, Catherine felt a slight resentment at having to share with them. She knew it was wrong, and even though she felt ashamed of herself, she couldn't seem to stop feeling like she gave away a piece of her privacy every time she sent a letter home, with or without pictures. Catherine knew it was unreasonable, and had long ago given up figuring out where the strange feelings came from. She was protective of her clan, but it was more than that. She did not want to share, plain and simple. Her daughters were something that she had done alone; one way she had excelled without her mother's influence. Even while she knew she was not being fair to her mother, Catherine's feelings of pulling away from her persisted. She was sure she could find the answer if she read enough books or asked the right people, but it never seemed like that big of a deal to the young mother. If she had been willing to admit it to herself, Catherine would have said the only person she could turn to for that answer was the one woman she so often resisted reaching out to. So, Catherine chose to not think about it too much. After all, between being a wife and mother and having her job, Catherine was a busy woman. There would be time later to ponder such deep thoughts; for now, she wanted to live her life her way.

Looking through the pictures brought a smile to Catherine's face. She could look at the lovely faces of her three daughters all day long. She loved the way she could tell what each of her daughters had been thinking at the time the camera captured the looks on their faces. Patricia, at almost 12, was a miniature version of herself. Catherine often wondered if she treated her oldest child more like a friend than a child. She hoped she was doing a good job with Patricia, who was clearly her father's favorite. Catherine loved watching Anthony interact with his firstborn; the two of them were more alike than either one knew. And Linda, at 7, was still Catherine's baby. She knew it was past time to wean her in so many ways. The child was certainly old enough to bathe herself and even wash her own hair, but Catherine knew once she gave up simple motherly tasks such as these, she would never have a chance to do them again. But even she had to admit that washing Linda's hair at the kitchen sink was starting to be a bit ridiculous. It had been fine when she was a baby, but now it was almost uncomfortable for both mother and daughter. Yet Catherine still refused to give up this task. Sarah was stuck in the middle at 10 years old. She and Patricia were such good friends, but sometimes the older kids on base came around persuading Patricia to find a way to exclude Sarah from their outings. This hurt Sarah terribly, but Catherine did not quite know how to fix her daughter's pain. Having had only brothers, she was not sure how to handle it when problems arose with her girls. Often she found herself offering time with Linda as a replacement for Patricia. Even when Sarah agreed to this plan, Catherine did not miss the look that crossed both faces of her daughters. Linda, so often left alone with no one to play with, was understandably thrilled at the thought of playing with one of her older sisters. Sarah did not feel the same way, but was polite enough most of the time to not let her true feelings show.

Catherine chose a few photos from the envelope she and the girls had picked up from the store, and pulled out a sheet of paper to start a letter for home. She told each of her girls to write a letter to their grandparents as well. They quickly found their stationery and got to work. Patricia chose a box with flowers embossed on the edges while Sarah had little puppies around the edges of her paper. Linda had a package of notebook paper in every color of the rainbow. While she was not technically using stationery, it was her favorite paper, and she spent a lot of time picking out the perfect color for her grandparents.

Catherine found it hard to write exactly what she wanted her mother and daddy to know. She needed them to hear that she was happy, needed them to see her as a grown woman more than capable of living her life away from them. She also wanted to be honest, but she knew how her mother worried. Life was not perfect, but when was it ever perfect for any of them? She saw no need to tell any of their challenges as a young family to her mother. She briefly thought her mother might be able to offer some sage advice, but quickly dismissed it. She had not lived at home for over 12 years, and there was no going back to the child she had been when she had lived with them.

Briefly, when her daughters were all just babies, she thought she had started a true friendship with her mother. But something always happened to bring Catherine back to reality. An innocent comment from her mother about what she was cooking for supper, or some unsolicited advice about how she was raising her girls. Or the way her mother never mentioned Anthony unless she brought him up first. These subtle clues had caused Catherine to realize she never would be anything but the baby of the family to her parents. This role did not bring her the joy it once had. For one thing, she often felt a sense of guilt. Even though they had never once mentioned it to her, and Catherine knew they never would, she knew in her heart they were disappointed in her. Getting pregnant before marriage meant a lot of different things to her family, none of them good. But, to their credit, they had never once let their disappointment show. Neither had Catherine. She had had her own dreams as a young girl. She had not planned on working at the hotel for very long. In fact, she was only working there to earn money to pay for college when she had the chance meeting at the store with Anthony that would change her life forever. These were now dreams she dare not share with anyone. Dreams best left alone. Dreams she had not even shared with Anthony because there was no reason to cause him any pain. She had settled into her life as a wife and mother. She was finding joy in her job at the bank. She needed to let her dreams from so long ago become what they were, part of her past.

Sealing the large envelope stuffed with letters and photographs, Catherine knew it would take several stamps to mail it. Each girl had written a letter in her own style. Their personalities shone through in each one. Catherine made sure to give her mother enough news to satisfy her, but she did not tell her anything too personal. Why should she? What if something else in her life was a source of disappointment for her parents? Hadn't she already done enough damage?

Ella grabbed the thick envelope Frank handed to her before he had a chance to sit down at the table. "Whoa, girl! I know you're excited, but you almost gave me a paper cut." He could not resist teasing her. He knew how much she looked forward to these letters from their youngest child. He also knew, more likely than not, that Ella would be sad for a few days after reading the letter. He read them too, and he never felt sad. He thought there must be something Catherine was not telling her momma, rather than the words she wrote, that was making his wife sad. For the life of him, he just couldn't figure it out, but he never had understood the ways of women. As much as he did not want to admit it, his little girl had grown into a woman. He tried not to focus on that too much. He had done a great job so far. After all, his little girl seemed happy. What more could he ask for?

Ella opened the letter and let the contents fall to the table. She greedily reached for the pictures first, almost crying as she saw the four beautiful faces around the Christmas tree. As always, she searched her daughter's face first, looking for any sign of unhappiness. Finding none as usual, she looked carefully at the faces of the three girls she loved more than life itself. How she wished they all lived closer. She was painfully aware of how much she was missing in their lives. She could only hope for a chance, one day, to spend time with them and to find a place within each of their hearts again. It was truly all she wanted out of life.

*

Ella put the photo back in the box. She knew a little bit more about her daughter now than she had when she first received it. Ella realized now, more than ever, that she had missed opportunities to truly talk to her child. She knew, given the chance again, she would push a little harder. She would not have spent so much time in silence if she had her life to live over.

Most importantly she knew her daughter was about to receive news that would change both of their worlds forever. And looking at the picture now lying on top of all the others, Ella wished she could go back in time and tell her to be a little more aggressive, to just try a little harder for answers. Would time have mattered? Ella had no way of knowing, but she sure wished for a second chance to find out.

Chapter Seven

The next day when Ella reached into the box, she knew she had to pull out more than just one picture. She knew how the next few years on her trip down memory lane were going to blend together. Maybe this time she could make more sense of it all, but she doubted it. It had not made sense to her then, and she had no reason to believe it would make sense to her now so many years later. Grabbing a handful of photos to take to the couch, Ella allowed her mind to drift back to the phone call she received not long after that package of letters and photos had been ripped by her from Frank's hands.

*

She answered the phone that Sunday, and was surprised to hear the voice of her daughter. She was delighted, but also alarmed. Even though it was Sunday and the rates were cheaper, none of them could afford to make long distance phone calls, so this was either very good news or very bad news. Either way, there was news worth sharing, worth spending the money a long distance phone call would cost. Ella did not plan to waste any of her precious daughter's minutes. "What's wrong?"she demanded, sounding harsher than she had intended.

"Oh Mother. Why do you assume something is wrong? Can't I just call home?" was Catherine's quick reply.

Rolling her eyes, even though she knew her daughter could not see her, Ella just waited for Catherine to continue. Hearing a sigh over the telephone line, Ella knew her daughter was a bit upset with her, but still she silently waited for her to continue.

"Well, Mother, I am calling to tell you and Daddy that Anthony got orders. And we're coming home!!"

Ella had to hold onto the wall to keep from falling over. Her face must have turned white because Frank rose from his chair to come stand over her. "What's wrong?"he mouthed. Instead of answering him, Ella told Catherine, "That's wonderful news! When will you be home?"

Things happened quickly after that. It turned out that while it was true they were all coming home, Anthony would only be staying a few weeks before being sent overseas for a year. Ella and Frank wondered if this meant they would be in charge of Catherine and the girls. Would they be living with them? They did not have to wonder for long. As soon as they moved home, the young family got set up in base housing. Catherine explained it was only temporary, stating she had to hunt for a house as soon as Anthony left.

Determined to impress her parents, she quickly found a house, bought it, and even waited alone outside the house one day as the movers carried all their belongings in for her. She set up house, and did so with gusto. Ella was smart enough to keep her mouth shut when Catherine put the dishes above the stove, even though she thought it was an inconvenient place to have to reach every night. She knew this was something her young daughter needed to do on her own, so she tried to keep a smile on her face at all times.

Catherine felt frustrated. Part of her wanted, in fact needed, her mother's help. But her mother just smiled, and offered no advice. Catherine supposed she should be very happy about this, but she couldn't help feeling just a little offended. What was wrong with her? Did she want to be her mother's child or not? She certainly could not have it both ways. She knew, in her heart, she was acting like a spoiled brat, but at least it didn't show. At least she hoped her mother could not see that deeply into her soul. Over the years, Catherine had lost the ability to see through her mother. It was like her mother had become a little less real to her every time they were together. Or maybe she had become more real. Catherine wasn't sure which one was true. All she did know was that her mother was no longer larger-than-life. Catherine had long since stopped thinking her mother had all the answers. This liberated her and frightened her at the same time. If her mother did not know all the answers, did anyone? And who would Catherine go to if she ever truly needed help? These were the type of questions that kept her up late into the night on more than one occasion. But, as was becoming more and more her response to life, she kept silent.

Ella enjoyed spending time with her daughter again. Watching Catherine and the girls start this new chapter of their life made Ella sad that her daughter had to manage these responsibilities without the help of her husband. She tried to understand Anthony's job, and the way the Air Force could take a man from his family for a full year, but none of it made any sense to Ella. After all, Frank made all her major decisions for her. The fact that Ella had never even learned to drive a car had rarely bothered her. There simply was no need to learn, she had Frank to drive her anywhere she wanted to go.

Spending time with Catherine and the girls after so much time apart forced Ella to tread softly. But still she could not help but feel as though her daughter wanted to tell her something. Every time they were together, she felt a tension that she had not expected to feel. She was not sure what to say, so she found herself saying nothing. At each visit, it became harder to even consider bringing up the uncomfortable silence that often hung between the two of them. And the girls were always running around, giving the two women the perfect excuse to talk about everything except the one thing they both desperately needed to say. Visit after visit left Ella feeling incomplete somehow. She would return home, and retreat into silence as she pondered the time she had spent with her daughter.

Days turned into weeks, and weeks turned into months. Ella had found a rhythm in her new life with Catherine and the girls. She loved the time they spent together, and learned a lot about them. Listening to the girls talk about their Wyoming home helped Ella understand the young ladies they were each growing into. Ella also knew Catherine was counting down to the day Anthony would be coming home. It would not be long now, and the two of them could at long last be together. Ella had never doubted their love, but seeing her daughter and the obvious way she missed her husband made Ella smile. In spite of the way the marriage had started, it was a good union. She wondered if Catherine knew how happy she was for her. As usual, she did not say anything, choosing to hide her feelings deep in her heart rather than share them with another person.

With only six weeks of separation left, Ella knew Catherine must be feeling excited, but every time they were together she only sensed an anxious sadness from her daughter. Finally, she had to speak up. In her uncharacteristic way, Ella asked Catherine if she wanted to tell her what was wrong. Her daughter's response was certainly not what she had expected. Catherine broke down and fell into her mother's arms. Ella, instantly alarmed, rubbed her daughter's back and waited for her to speak.

"Oh Mother. Something is wrong, but I don't know what it is. Since I've been home, I've been going to the doctors on base. They keep telling me different things, but my problem just won't go away. I can't fight this fear that's growing in me that something might really be wrong. I feel so alone. The doctors seem to want to push me out of the room as soon as I get in there, and with Anthony gone, I just have no one to talk to about this."

Ella felt like Catherine had slapped her across the face, but she did not want her daughter to know how much her words had hurt her. "Talk to me, Catherine. Tell me what has been going on and maybe I can help."

"Oh Mother. I didn't want to worry you." As Catherine revealed to her mother the extent of the doctor visits, Ella indeed found herself more worried than she had ever been. Something was wrong with her little girl, and the answers from the doctors just did not add up.

"You actually had a doctor tell you to switch lotions? And then another one suggested your bra was too tight? Oh honey, here's what you need to do. You need to go see one more doctor, and don't leave his office until you get an answer. Tell him everything you just told me. Ask him to treat you like he would treat his own wife or daughter. And pray. We both need to be on our knees praying every night."

After a day in her momma's arms, Catherine felt stronger that night than she had in a long time. She took out a sheet of paper and a calendar to start taking notes for her next visit to the doctor's office. She planned to take her mother's advice and be prepared. She also planned to lean on her mother's strength and refuse to leave the doctor without answers. She felt like time was running out, as there were just a few weeks left before her husband would be home. They had a new chapter in their life opening up, and Catherine did not want any lingering medical concerns to come between them and their happiness as a family.

*

Ella looked at the photos on her lap. None of them could have known what the future held for Catherine and her family. Ella wanted more than anything to go back in time, to somehow climb into the pictures with her daughter and her sweet family. She wished she had known earlier of her daughter's silent suffering. She could not help but think she could have offered some degree of comfort if Catherine had only let her in sooner.

But at least Catherine had finally let her in. And Ella found herself crying as she thought of how she had gotten the chance she had been wanting for so long. She cried, remembering the closeness mother and daughter had found again, and the horrible reason they were able to find their way back into each other's arms and each other's hearts.

Chapter Eight

Thinking back to the first day her daughter had revealed her

many visits to the doctor caused Ella to painstakingly go back over

the days that had followed. She wondered, even now years later, if

she should have forced her daughter to talk to her sooner. Was her

silence partly to blame for her daughter's diagnosis? She wondered,

as she had so many times before, if she should have gone with her

to the doctor that day. She tried to fight the lingering feeling that

something could have made a difference. Had God determined long

ago where Catherine's story would end? Were any of them ever in

control of any of it? From the day the doctor told Ella she had

conceived to the last time she saw her daughter, had it all been part

of a bigger plan, one in place long before Ella had ever even considered having children? These were the kind of thoughts that kept Ella up night after night. These were the questions she knew she would never have answered in this lifetime. But these were also the questions she never could put far out of her mind. She supposed that was the way with the bond between a mother and a daughter. Catherine had always been a part of Ella, and she always would be.

Picking up a new stack of photographs, Ella wondered why she had started this project. Surely she had known it would bring about pain. Any time you pulled at a sore, you were left with a stinging feeling reminiscent of what had caused the injury in the first place. But just like a child who picked at a scab until the bleeding started again despite being constantly told not to, this story was one Ella forced herself to visit again and again. Somehow she owed it to her daughter, and always had.

Ella pulled a picture from the stack of photos and just stared at it for a long time. Looking at this picture of Catherine revealed her story. As she sat on a couch with a scarf on her head, it did not take much imagination to see the cancer patient she had become.

Snuggled in close to her was Linda. Catherine had a protective arm around her daughter. The picture showed both the innocence of the child and the rapidly disappearing innocence of the mother. There was an obvious anguish on Catherine's face that Ella wished she had never seen there. She knew in her heart how helpless and hopeless her daughter had felt on that day. On all the days of her sickness actually. Ella could not forget how brave her daughter had been, choosing to suffer so much in silence for the sake of those she loved.

*

Following her mother's advice, Catherine had refused to leave the doctor's office that day until he ran tests. She had her notes with her, with specific dates and well-documented symptoms. Maybe this had impressed the doctor. Or maybe he just found the puzzle intriguing. None of that mattered. What did matter was the fact that he seemed to be taking her seriously. When he looked at her, Catherine could tell he truly saw her. This was the first doctor who had treated her that way, and it felt good to be seen. After the tests were run, the doctor explained, "Mrs. Williams, we have to wait for the results. I simply cannot give you an answer today as much as I want to. Please let me call you in as soon as I hear back the results. And try not to worry. We just don't have any answers until we get the test results, but I think I'll know something by early next week." Catherine thanked the doctor, and left his office. She liked this man, and she could tell he truly cared about her. And the timing certainly felt right. She had a babysitter scheduled to keep the three girls starting next Wednesday. When she picked Anthony up from the airport, she had planned a three-day getaway for them. It would be the honeymoon they had never had. It would certainly be a surprise to her husband, but one she was sure he would be pleased with.

Although they wrote frequently, it had not been possible to talk on the phone while he had been away this past year. As much as she longed for him to hold her in his arms, she also really just wanted to hear the deep timbre of his voice. She had missed him terribly. She had kept her news from him about her health. He could not come home unless it was serious, and so far she had simply spent a few months going to see various doctors. When she found out the news next week, she would have plenty of time to tell him then. She could see him now, chiding her softly for letting herself get so worked up over nothing. He would call her his little worrywart as he kissed the top of her head. The problem would be fixed, and they would move on.

Their girls were getting older, and Catherine was finally back home with her family. It felt right somehow knowing her girls would turn into young women with the influence of their grandparents in their lives. It had taken her some time, but she had come to realize that she needed help raising her children. She didn't feel like she would resist their help now like she would have just a few years ago. She knew her girls could learn things from her parents that they could not learn from her and Anthony. Besides, it would be nice to have some alone time with her husband. Starting their life together the way they had, there had not been much of a chance for the two of them to spend any time alone. Catherine had often regretted that she had never had a true honeymoon with her husband. Yes, Catherine was certain next week would be the beginning of a special time in their lives. One they would look back on fondly. It would be a time of growing closer as a couple and as a family. While she wasn't exactly ready to go home and pack her bags for their trip yet, Catherine had a good feeling about the test results. The doctor had shown no concern, only care for her as a person. She left his office feeling lighter than she had in the past several weeks.

Not wanting to concern her mother, Catherine shut her out again. She figured she could just call her the next week with the good test results, letting them all put it behind them. She felt strong. She would never have thought she could go through any kind of battle without Anthony, but this year had proven to her that she was more self-sufficient than she had ever known. It felt good. But, if she admitted the whole truth, she was ready to be under the protective cover of her man again. It would actually feel good to have someone take some of the burden from her shoulders. It would be nice to not have to think through every decision alone, often second-guessing herself to the point of feeling physically sick.

The weekend flew by as Catherine and the girls cleaned the house and yard in anticipation of Anthony's return. The girls made cute signs to tape to the front windows, so the first thing he would see at his new home was an outpouring of their love. Catherine hoped he would like the house she had chosen for their family. She never would have believed she could pick out a home, much less buy it, on her own, but she had. Her strength had impressed her on a deep level. She was certain her husband would be impressed as well.

On Monday, the girls went shopping with their mother. Catherine knew she needed a well-stocked pantry for the babysitter. She also wanted to cook a few meals so the girls would not have to rely on sandwiches or soup from a can. As they were laughing and putting away the groceries, the phone rang. Catherine answered it on the third ring, and was instantly happy to hear the lady on the other end of the line announce she was calling from the doctor's office. In the calm detached voice of the medical profession, the lady simply asked Catherine if she would be free to come in tomorrow at 2:00 to discuss the test results. Catherine quickly agreed. She was thrilled. The doctor had done exactly as he said he would, and the timing continued to be perfect. It seemed like such a positive sign to Catherine. She could not wait to put all of this behind her.

At noon the next day as the little family of girls ate their lunch, Catherine broached the subject of her doctor's appointment. Since Patricia was now almost 15 years old, it was impossible to keep much from her. Catherine simply told the girls the test results were back, and by supper that night they would have some answers. When Patricia saw no fear in her mother's eyes, she inwardly breathed a sigh of relief. She offered to make spaghetti. She had been trying to figure out the secret to her mother's amazing sauce, and tonight gave her the perfect excuse to try to cook it in the manner her mom had for all these years. They had actually had a few spaghetti contests over the past year, and Patricia was ready to finally win one. Laughing at her daughter's excitement over cooking supper, Catherine agreed, kissing all three of her children good-bye as she left to run a few errands before seeing the doctor.

Arriving shortly before her 2:00 appointment, Catherine let the receptionist know she had arrived. She still was not nervous as she sat down and started thumbing through the stack of magazines on the small table in the doctor's waiting area. The one with Robert Redford on the cover caught her eye, and she was soon reading about the man she enjoyed watching on the big screen. The article was so good she didn't hear the nurse at first. "Catherine Williams? You may come back now. The doctor is ready to see you." Hearing her name, Catherine reluctantly put down her magazine. She briefly considered slipping it into her purse so she could read it later at home, but she knew her mother would not approve. "Funny to think of disappointing my mother now," thought Catherine as she followed the nurse down the short hallway to an exam room.

Opening the door for her, the nurse explained the doctor was on his way. Catherine sat on the crinkly paper and waited. She looked around at the white walls, and wondered why the doctor hadn't bothered to put up any paintings. Before she could get too far with that train of thought, a light knock alerted her to the doctor's presence. Trying to read his expression proved to be an exercise in futility. This doctor had apparently delivered a lot of news to people over the years, and had learned to keep his expression neutral. Still, Catherine did not feel uneasy in the least.

"Mrs. Williams, We ran several tests, and I have the results. I'm very sorry to have to share this with you, but the tests indicate I don't have the best news to share. Have you ever heard of inflammatory breast cancer? I'm so sorry to have to tell you the test results reveal you have this rare and aggressive form of this disease."

Before the doctor could add any more, Catherine asked him the question she had not known was in her heart until that very moment, "My girls. Doctor, can my girls get this from me?"

The doctor smiled a sad smile as he explained that, in his experience, this was not likely to be passed on to her daughters. He explained how the dimpling of the skin on her breasts that other doctors had attributed to a brand of lotion or a type of bra was actually an unusual symptom of a rare disease. He told her how sorry he was to tell her such bad news. He explained she should make preparations because, in his opinion, she only had three months left to get her affairs in order.

All Catherine could think while the doctor was going on and on in his kind voice was, "I'm 35 years old. I have a husband and three young girls. Who will care for my family if I really only have three months to live?"

Catherine left the doctor's office in a haze. The doctor slipped a card into her hand with her next appointment date written on it. They had already discussed treatment options, but Catherine was not sure how much of it she could repeat if she were forced to. She kept seeing three faces through her haze of tears. She saw her sweet daughters, at home right now waiting for her, planning to eat supper together while hearing about her doctor's appointment and the test results. There was no way her girls were ready for the truth.

None of them were prepared, simply because she, as their mother, had not prepared them. The guilt Catherine felt was overwhelming.

Catherine quietly let herself in the front door of their small home. Patricia, the only one close enough to hear her mother come in the door, called out a greeting. She met her mother halfway between the stove and the front door, dropping the spoon she had been using to stir the spaghetti sauce as soon as she saw her mother's face. Unable to hear even one word from her mom, Patricia ran out the front door and into their yard. Catherine felt helpless as she watched her go. Sarah and Linda had heard the spoon fall, and both came rushing from the living room into the kitchen. Sarah's face registered alarm as she took in her mom's puffy red eyes. To Catherine, the saddest reaction of all was on the face of her youngest daughter. At nine years old, she was an innocent, and was simply glad her mommy was home. Running to her mom, Linda wrapped both arms around her waist and looked up at her through smudged glasses. The tears started flowing down

Catherine's cheeks then, and she quickly got all three of her girls settled on the couch.

Looking each of them in the eyes for several seconds before she spoke, she told them her news. "Girls, I didn't get the news I wanted to get. But you are all fine. Please understand the doctor assured me this is not something I'll pass on to you."

Patricia was appalled at the direction of her mother's thoughts and quickly said, "Mom, just tell us. What did the doctor say?"

When Catherine told her girls she had breast cancer, the air seemed to leave the room. As they all cried, she looked up from the couch toward the ceiling and silently asked, "God, how will I ever go to the airport tomorrow and tell Anthony?"

*

Ella remembered that day well as she held the photo of her daughter and Linda. She remembered how Catherine had made a last minute decision to send someone else to the airport to tell Anthony about the cancer diagnosis she had received and then to bring him home to her. Knowing the pain her daughter had been in, Ella once again questioned her reluctance to push her daughter to take that planned honeymoon they had dreamed of for years even if it meant Catherine had to share the bad news with her husband herself.

Missing her daughter like she did every day of her life, Ella fell asleep holding tightly to that precious photograph. She prayed for her granddaughters, like she also did every night, as she drifted off to sleep.

Chapter Nine

Ella woke in the middle of the night feeling more alone than she had in several years. She found herself thinking about her granddaughters, and where their lives had taken them. She knew Catherine would be proud of each of them. As she often did, she wondered if she had missed any opportunities to help the girls. She had tried to be there for them during their mother's sickness as well as after. As always, she just did not know if she had been what they needed. She knew she never would know. Wondering why the past tormented her and if it always would, she drifted back to sleep for a while.

When the sun rose a few hours later, Ella was already on the couch with several photos from the old box in her lap. She took her time looking at each one, enjoying the background of each picture as much as the people in them. She found she could learn a lot by looking at the setting of each picture instead of just focusing on those smiling up at the camera. She also knew she needed a diversion from looking at the face of her sick daughter. It still hurt to see what cancer had done to her precious girl.

Each time Ella had looked at these pictures over the years, she had discovered something new. She knew the first time she saw them years ago, she had only noticed her daughter and her children. After all, in those days, she was selfish, often feeling sorry for herself and trying to find solace in their faces. Ella had wanted more time with her daughter and her family, and she often found herself feeling left out. She would find herself fighting hard to keep those feelings from turning into a full-blown depression. Most of all, she had to keep Frank from finding out. She knew he would never understand. And she knew she did not have the ability to make him completely feel what she was feeling. Suspecting he might actually feel a little of what she too felt, Ella chose to keep quiet. She did not want to add to his pain, so she never told him hers.

Looking at one picture made Ella wonder who had been behind the camera.

*

Catherine was in bed, looking comfortable enough although her bald head gave away what the cancer was doing to her body. She had invested in several wigs and scarves, but had stopped wearing them at home after the day Linda walked in on her and discovered her mom had lost all of her hair. Catherine had wanted to spare this reality from her youngest daughter, but she simply forgot to lock her bedroom door that one day. Linda, with her usual exuberance, had rushed in to tell her mother something that had happened earlier at school. Of course, she stopped talking as soon as she saw her mother's bald head. Catherine had wondered if Linda even understood what it all meant. Her greatest wish was that she wouldn't die before Linda was old enough to understand it all. This was a prayer she prayed almost as often as she asked God to take the cancer away.

*

Looking closer at the picture, Ella noticed the stacks of books on the table beside her daughter's bed. How Ella wished for a way to see the titles of the books. She wondered what her daughter had been reading in her final days. What had held her attention? What, if anything, had been a source of comfort to her? She knew she would have someone drive her to a bookstore so she could buy every single book if she only knew the titles of them. Then she would devour them, just to feel closer to her daughter once more. She would give anything for more time with her daughter, even if it was only by reading some of the same words she had once read.

For the first time Ella wondered if Anthony had taken the picture. Catherine certainly was smiling in a special way, and Ella suspected that particular smile was one she reserved for her husband alone. Ella had not allowed herself to dwell on that when she first saw the picture even though she had to have recognized the look since she herself reserved a similar one for her own husband. But now she hungrily searched for clues in the pictures. She desperately wanted to understand everything about her daughter's much-too-short life.

Each picture did unveil new clues. Ella saw the poem written in calligraphy and hanging in a frame on a wall in the background of one of the pictures. She remembered when Catherine had first shown it to her, and she was ashamed to think about her reaction.

*

"Mother, look what I made for Anthony. I plan to give it to him on our anniversary. What do you think?"

After reading the poem, Ella said to her daughter, "The calligraphy is beautiful. Where did you learn to do that?"

While Catherine gladly answered her mother's question, it was not the reaction she had hoped for. Ella knew how she had made her daughter feel, but she could not quite bring herself to acknowledge the lovely message the poem conveyed. It had been a good poem, one that any husband would be thrilled to hear his wife speak over him. Ella was certain Anthony would be overjoyed, and she was astounded by her daughter's talent. But she just did not want to talk about her daughter's love life. As much as she refused to admit it to anyone, even herself, part of her still resented Anthony after all these years. Her daughter had been ripped from her arms, never to find her way back to them again. And Ella blamed Anthony for that. She did not welcome them, but the feelings were there just the same.

Catherine sighed as she put the framed poem back into the closet. She would wrap it up in some nice paper and tie it with a ribbon later. She was certain she would still be alive on their anniversary. She had been feeling better lately, and was well past the three-month death sentence the doctor had spoken over her. Passing that milestone had liberated her somehow. She felt alive in a way she could not quite explain. She knew she was not cured, but she felt a peace that had been missing when she had been first diagnosed.

She thought about the words in her poem. She had written about the part of her husband that was hers and hers alone. She truly felt she knew Anthony in a way no one else ever had or ever would. And she wanted him to know. In fact, she wanted everyone else to know too. There weren't words to explain to her daughters the love between their mom and dad. She only hoped the poem would somehow help them understand. And she also hoped her three young girls would remember this poem as they each tried to find their own true love. Catherine knew she had found her soul mate, and she knew that was the one gift she would be honored to share with each of her girls.

As Catherine turned from the closet, she went back into the livingroom where her mother waited on the couch. She wished there was a way for them to truly talk. They talked around most topics, neither one of them quite knowing how to say the words they really wanted to let flow. Why was it so hard to talk to her mother? When had this wall come up between the two of them?

Since Ella could not drive, Catherine knew she would need to give her mother a lift home soon. She felt a little guilty that she was ready to have her house back to herself. She had built a good home for her husband and children, and she was proud of every room. She knew she would never be the cook her mother was, and she was certain there was more dust in her house than had ever been on any surface of her mother's home, but, as she looked around, she saw memories. She had been the one to make this house their home. And she knew her family would agree with her.

When someone walked in the front door, the first thing to be seen was a mirror hanging on the wall. Catherine loved that mirror. She loved the way everyone who entered her home had a chance to see their own happiness reflected back as they came in for a visit. If her visitor turned to the left, he entered the dining room and kitchen as well as a den Anthony had added on after he got home from his year away. A turn to the right would reveal the living area with a hall leading to the bedrooms and bathrooms. It was a small, cozy home. Catherine loved every inch of it. She felt like the queen of her very own castle. Since her illness, Anthony had tried to find things to give to her to make her happy. A pool was now set up in the backyard. This addition thrilled the children, and it made Catherine smile. There was a small camper back there too, a promise of trips to come for the young family. A promise of a future.

Catherine was thinking of this future as she asked her mother if she was ready to return home. As the two women drove away in near silence, Catherine thought of how she was leaving her future behind and heading straight toward her past. She loved her mother; she truly did, but somehow her mother made her think too much about how things used to be. Catherine was happy she had been able to leave the home of her parents and what it represented. She also knew she had to find a way to make her peace with her mother before it was too late even if that meant reliving her past.

*

As Ella looked through the rest of the photographs, she felt a pang of regret. Why hadn't she told Catherine how lovely her poem was? Why had she never given her daughter the opening to brag about her husband and all he meant to her? She realized now how her silence had hurt her daughter. She knew she had missed other opportunities too that, once gone, could never be reclaimed.

Ella was glad that she had finally figured out the great love story that was her daughter and her husband. Her only regret was that she had figured it out after it was too late to share Catherine's joy with her. Could she have learned more about her daughter if she had allowed them to have conversations about Anthony? Regret made Ella's chest grow tight as she thought about how she should have been a different mother to her daughter.

Feeling her knees protest with pain, Ella slowly rose from the couch. It was time to put the photos away for the day. She would open the closet door, drop the photos in the box, and then leave them behind the door in darkness. But Ella knew she could never keep her memories behind a closed door. They were with her a little more every day it seemed. She wondered if she would ever be free of them. She was starting to wonder if she even wanted to be free.

At 80 years old, Ella was realizing she had a lot left to learn. She hoped she had enough time. She knew she could not go back to her past, but she was starting to think maybe there was a way she could be a better mother to Catherine now, even so many years after her death.

Chapter Ten

Ella was seeing things a little differently as she looked through the old photographs. When she woke up this morning, she realized that she was starting to discover a truth about her past that she had not been aware of before. This gave her a reason to get out of bed, and start on her task for the day. It was like a veil was lifting, and she was seeing clearly for the first time in a long time, maybe ever.

As she often did, Ella wished she could share these pictures with Frank. He had seen them before he died, but he never really looked at pictures the same way she did. He would give each one a cursory glance, and maybe even mumble a platitude, but he never really was one to have a long discussion about a photograph. In fact, Ella was not sure Frank had ever thought they were of much value. She smiled to herself as she imagined what he would say about her new adventure. She was sure he would mention there were better ways for his wife to spend her time. But she knew he had always meant well. And she knew she might be wrong too. Catherine's death had hit her daddy hard; chances were good that if Frank were alive he would be on this couch looking at these pictures with his wife. They held memories, and she knew more than most that those are not ever to be wasted. Ella choked back a sob as she thought about how she had learned this particular lesson the hard way.

Ella found a picture of Catherine sitting outside under their carport. She knew it must have been Easter or maybe Mother's Day. Everyone was wearing bright clothes, and the children all had on pretty dresses and hats. She remembered the days when her family would come over for lunch and then retire outside to sit under the carport. The meals had been huge, prepared entirely by Ella. Those were good days. Ella could not remember the last time she prepared a meal for others or sat outside just to enjoy the breeze. She wondered what it would be like to go sit under her carport alone.

She didn't think she wanted to find out. Somehow she knew, no matter how lovely the weather was, the memories would suffocate her.

Ella thought Catherine seemed happy enough in the picture, but she noticed how tired her daughter's eyes had looked. Her hair was growing back in, so Catherine was not wearing a scarf around her head. Ella could tell her daughter's black hair was soft and downy like a baby's. She wondered if she had even touched it back then. She knew she would give anything for one more chance to touch her daughter, to hug her and tell her how much she was loved. Ella nearly doubled over in pain as this thought caused more memories to roll over her. She remembered Catherine as the tiny baby she brought home from the hospital in her arms. She thought about the young girl she would let stand on her feet as they sang together and danced around the house until they were both dizzy. She even remembered the teenager who would still allow her to hold her sometimes, but not very often. When was the last time she hugged her child? How many times had she held her between the day

Anthony drove her away from home and the day her daughter had died alone in a sterile hospital room? The guilt was almost more than Ella could bear. She forced herself to look at the picture again, and focus on remembering the happy day that the family had spent together. No, she probably had not held Catherine that day, but she knew in her heart she had done her best to make the day perfect for her.

*

Catherine tried to make herself comfortable in the hard metal chair. She knew her parents liked sitting outside, but she sure wished someone would suggest they all go back inside where the couch was soft and the air conditioner was running. Catherine knew she was not going to be the one to bring it up. One thing cancer had taught her was that everyone did everything in their power to try to make her comfortable. So much so that sometimes she just felt like screaming. She almost wished someone would be rude to her or get mad at her. It would make her feel human again. Catherine knew these kinds of thoughts were irrational, but she really did not care.

She was hot and sore and nearing exhaustion. And she was really tired of having to keep a smile pasted on her face. She knew everyone was trying to talk about everything except the one topic they all had on their minds, and it was about to drive her crazy.

What would they think if she just started talking about breast cancer? Maybe throw in a few comments about chemotherapy and how it made her vomit until she thought she would die. Until she wanted to die if she were being honest with everyone and herself. Maybe she should tell them about the radiation treatments. Or about going bald, and the horror she saw reflected in the eyes of her children when they saw their mother without hair for the first time. There were so many awful things she could say, and maybe she needed to say them, but she sat there with that smile pasted on her face as her mother went on and on about some distant cousin no one wanted to talk about. Catherine knew her mother was doing her best to make it a nice day for everyone, but she wished for once she would just be real. She wanted her mother to ask her how she was doing, and then really listen as Catherine poured it all out of her.

But she knew her mother wouldn't ask, just like she knew she would never tell her.

Sometimes Catherine thought she would explode. If only she could give a little of the pain away, maybe she could keep going. But she knew better than to share her pain with her mother. If she wanted to know, wouldn't she ask? Although Catherine knew the answer to that question, she had to fight to not let resentment build up. She knew her mother loved her. She had to wonder what she would be feeling if one of her daughters had been given the death sentence of breast cancer. That thought sobered Catherine up. She knew she would be behaving just like her mother was. For the first time, Catherine really looked at her. The pain was there. It was in the new lines around her mother's eyes. It was in the gray hair on her mother's head. It was there in the way her mother flitted around trying desperately to make everything perfect. Catherine smiled a sad little smile as she saw her mother's love for her. She still wished they could talk about it, but she understood now that talking might be the one thing that would make her mother's world finally come crashing down. No, Catherine knew her mother was struggling to hold it together, and she certainly did not plan to be the one to make her fall apart.

Catherine caught her mother's eye and smiled. Feeling her breath catch in her throat, Ella smiled back at her baby girl. The tears came, but Ella controlled them. She jumped up to get everyone more lemonade, but the truth was she had to escape Catherine. She could not, would not, break down today. Catherine seemed to be feeling well, and the girls were happy. There would be no talk of cancer on this day if Ella could help it. Sure, she had a lot of questions for her daughter. But, if she were being honest, she did not want to hear the answers. She was scared to death that her daughter was dying. She did not want to know the details. She preferred to live in denial, believing some miracle would happen and make this entire cancer thing go away. As a mother, she could not bear the thought of losing her baby.

*

Ella put the photo down. She saw a lot more in the picture now than she had the day it was taken. She wondered why she had not found a way to talk to her daughter. Maybe that particular day would not have been a good time for them to have a conversation, but Ella could have found a time if she had wanted to. Why had she let her fear control her? Had her daughter gone to her death needing a mother to talk to? These thoughts were heavy on Ella's heart as she got up from her knees and made her way into her bed.

Like she did every night, Ella had spent some quiet time with her Lord. She asked Him about her daughter as usual. She never heard Him actually speak to her, but she was starting to feel like maybe He was part of this photo project. Maybe it had been by His urging that she would finally peel back the layers of her life to find the peace which had eluded her for far too long.

Chapter Eleven

Ella rushed out of bed the next morning, anxious to see her daughter. Her night had been full of dreams so realistic, she almost expected to wake up and hear her daughter's voice. She knew better, just like she knew looking at pictures was not the same as actually seeing her daughter again. However, at her age, Ella rejoiced in the fact that she was closer than ever to seeing her last child when death finally came to claim her too. She did not care if today was that day. But she also knew, in her heart, she still had work to do.

As she grabbed the box of photographs with her now shaky hands, she knew what her plan for the day had to be. She needed to find every picture of her daughter in her final months. She wanted to put them in order, if she could figure out the dates by clues in the pictures. She needed desperately to see her child's face in each of these pictures. Seeing Catherine's face as her death got closer would let Ella know if her daughter had been feeling dread or embracing her death with peace. Ella desperately needed to know this, and she needed to know it today.

*

Catherine was getting sicker. She could feel something happening inside her body. She didn't think she looked any different on the outside, but she finally knew in her heart that she was truly dying. She watched life go on around her, but she felt as though hers had already stopped. She hated this feeling. She wanted desperately to be a part of what was going on with her family, but she found herself sitting on the sidelines more and more. Even when she was present, she was not really engaged. She wondered if her family could tell yet. She fought with everything in her to keep it from them. She knew losing her would be a pain all of them would carry with them forever, and she wanted to keep that pain from them as long as possible. There seemed to be less and less she could do for her family, but this was one final gift she could give to them.

As she painstakingly prepared to celebrate her parents' fiftieth anniversary, Catherine found herself tearing up, thinking about how she would not live to see her own silver anniversary, much less her golden. She would not see any of her golden years. She forced herself to travel this dreary path alone, acknowledging the fact she would never see her own grandchildren. She hoped to live long enough to see Patricia turn 18, Sarah 16, and Linda to turn the path toward womanhood. She did not think she was setting her goals too high. A lot of time had passed since the dreaded three-month mark that had been her death sentence. In fact, she was getting close to the three-year anniversary of her diagnosis. She knew every day was a gift, and she intended to treat each one as such.

So, she prepared a simple party, with gold-colored plates, napkins, and cutlery. She made a cake, and prepared a bowl of punch. It would be a surprise for her parents, with all the family in attendance. As Catherine put the final touches on the table, she heard Patricia call out, "Mom, look up!" The next thing she knew, she saw a flash and heard the click of the camera.

"Patricia, go take your grandparents' picture. After all, it's their party."

She watched a soft smile cover the face of her near-grown daughter, and listened as she explained, "I will. But I'm taking pictures right now of what's important. You look so pretty and happy. I just had to take your picture, Mom." As usual, her oldest daughter knew the right thing to say. In many ways, Patricia was like a friend to Catherine. She was grateful for the maturity she was seeing because she had a feeling Patricia would be taking over the role of mother soon.

Shaking her head to remove any more thoughts of death, Catherine took one last look at the table and joined her family for the celebration. She planned to lavish love on the two people who had given her life, and so much more over the years. She wanted today to be a perfect day for them.

The day after the party, Catherine was truly exhausted, barely able to get out of bed. At 37 years old, she knew a simple party should not have affected her this way, but she also knew her age had nothing to do with it. The real culprit was the disease that ate away a little more of her each day. She could almost feel it happening. It frightened her terribly, and keeping silent about it ate away at her almost as much as the cancer did. She wished yet again she had someone to talk to about it. Someone who could comfort her, and at least try to make it all better for her. She, of course, knew who the perfect person was for that job. The same person who had placed a cool cloth on her head every time she had been sick as a child. The same person who had made her soup and crackers smothered with grape jelly when she had been laid up in bed with a cold. She had so many memories of times her mother had taken care of her. Even though she knew how much her mother loved her, she just couldn't bring herself to pour out her pain to her. Knowing her mother would do everything in her power to make her feel better wasn't enough to make her pick up the phone; Catherine simply found it hard to ask for help. She didn't want to spend a lot of time examining why she felt that way. It seemed like it would take more effort than she could afford to give.

A few days later, on a Saturday, Catherine finally had enough energy to go about her daily activities. Saturdays had been her favorite day for as long as she could remember. Their life as a family had a wonderful rhythm. The week was for work for her and Anthony as well as school for the girls. But the weekends were for family time. Saturday was always chore day, but she knew her girls would agree with her that it was the best day of the week. Catherine was proud of how she had turned a mundane day of chores into a day the four girls of the family looked forward to. Anthony spent the day outside working in the yard or sometimes tinkering away in the workshop he had built for himself. She was proud of her husband, and the way he could make something out of nothing. Just like she could take a dirty house, put on some music, and turn a day of cleaning into a day of fun with her girls. Catherine knew now it was about more than entertaining them; it was about making memories. As she felt her end coming near, she listened to the songs more carefully each Saturday. It was her hope that her daughters, many years from now, would hear one of these songs and think of her. She knew it was selfish, but she wanted her girls to think of her every day for the rest of their lives. But she didn't want to tell them that. If there was a way to keep them from shouldering any extra burdens, she would give that one last gift to them.

Catherine looked up from her dusting when she heard the front door open. She was surprised to see Anthony standing there with tears in his eyes. "Honey, is something wrong?"

"No, I just wanted to come inside and see what my girls were up to." At this, all three girls looked up from their cleaning, wondering what was wrong. Their dad loved to work in the yard, and did not come in until every job was finished. And they knew it was too early for him to be finished.

"In fact, I want you girls to do me a favor. Will you sit on the couch with your mother?" At this, all four went and sat on the couch, each wondering silently what was really going on with him.

Anthony walked past them, and disappeared down the hall. He was back in a few seconds with the camera in his hand and a smile on his face.

"Oh, Anthony, we look a mess. You can take our picture later." At this, a solemn hush covered the room as Catherine's words sunk in. Everyone in the room knew there would not be much time left for moments like these. As each girl smiled outwardly while her heart was breaking a little more on the inside, Anthony took several shots.

"There, that should do it. I'm going back outside now." He set down the camera, and let himself out the door without looking back.

With that, Anthony was gone, and the girls slowly got up and resumed their cleaning. Catherine thought about the picture her husband had just taken. She no longer considered what she looked like. She thought ahead many years to a time when she knew her girls would see the picture and remember this day. A day was all she could be sure of having. She wanted to make sure each one with her girls would be one they would remember. So, she did a little dance as she made her way over to the stereo to turn up the music. As Simon and Garfunkel blared through the speakers, she continued her impromptu dance. Noticing the way Sarah was managing to smile a little even as she rolled her eyes at her mom, Catherine knew her plan had worked. She had always had fun with her girls, and they all four had laughed together a lot over the years. This was how she wanted them to remember her. She couldn't do a thing about the way this disease was making her look, and she knew her daughters would suffer torment from their memories of her sickness for years, maybe forever. She knew cancer was slowly taking her away just like she knew the end of her life would not be filled with dancing. She needed to plant these memories in her daughters' minds now; she could only hope they would help erase the memories she knew would soon be made for her precious children. She could not allow herself to think about how her death would affect them.

*

Ella put the pictures aside. She had seen enough for one day. The thing that jumped out at her the most was the vulnerable look in her daughter's eyes. She looked like a scared little girl in some of the pictures. Even though Ella could clearly see this now, she simply did not remember her daughter looking that way. In fact, Catherine always seemed so strong, right up to the end when cancer made her unable to speak. For the first time, she thought about the possibility that her daughter had chosen to die alone that day in the hospital. She had always felt a sense of guilt, knowing no one had been with her daughter when she breathed her final breath. Maybe Catherine had somehow planned it that way to save her family from the added grief of watching her die. She knew she would never know if this was true, or even possible, but this was the kind of selfless behavior that had always made her proud of her daughter.

Ella was starting to realize her daughter had let her see what she wanted her to see. At first, Ella was hurt by this, but as she had spent the day with the pictures, she again realized her daughter had given her a gift. It had cost her dearly, but she had protected her mother from the pain and fear she herself had been going through. She had kept quiet to keep her mother from pain. Ella knew her daughter had grown to be the woman she had always hoped she would be. She only wished she had figured it out sooner. It would have been wonderful to have seen the look on Catherine's face when she told her how proud she was of her.

Chapter Twelve

Ella woke up thinking it could not possibly be morning yet. After a fitful night of sleep, she really wanted to just stay under the covers and sleep the day away. But who did that at her age? Sometimes she felt every one of her years, but then there were the times she still felt like a young woman. Today was a mix of the two with her body feeling very old, but her mind reminding her of the young woman she had once been.

Slipping on her house shoes and her robe, Ella found her way to the bathroom. She looked in the mirror, letting her eyes take in what time had done to her body. She looked old, full of wrinkles. She took in her wiry gray hair and wondered how it had gotten so thin. If she closed her eyes, she could see a younger reflection. But she knew she would eventually have to open her eyes and face reality.

She also knew going back to the box of photos today meant facing another reality. She was not quite ready to do this, so she finished up in the bathroom and made her way to the kitchen. After making herself a cup of instant coffee, she settled into Frank's old chair at their small kitchen table. Although she rarely allowed herself to do so, today Ella let the memories of her husband take hold. She could see herself at the stove, making pancakes for her husband as he watched her over his cup of coffee. She could still see the way his eyes had subtly smiled at her, and how she had always known exactly what he was thinking. Their love affair had been a quiet one, without need for many words. She wondered now if that had been a good thing. She wished, not for the first time, that Frank had been more willing to talk about what had been going on with Catherine. Instead Ella had kept all her thoughts and feelings bottled up inside her, bearing her burden silently. She had done so to spare Frank pain. She wondered now if talking about Catherine would have helped both of them ease their pain a little.

As Ella shuffled to the closet to get the box, she thought of the way silence had followed her throughout her life. As a child, she had been taught to be seen but not heard. As a young wife, she understood her husband's word was final, and she learned to never question him. And, as a mother, she had learned to pick her battles. She chose to remain silent a lot for the sake of her children. Maybe she should have talked more. Had her silence been passed on to Catherine? Is that why she was trying, so many years later, to figure her daughter out by looking at pictures? Pictures could not talk back, Ella realized, as she picked up a stack and made her way to the couch.

Putting the pictures back in order as she had the day before, Ella settled in to look for more clues. This task had been easier than she had thought because it was obvious how the disease had ravaged her young daughter's body. Ella did not need to turn the pictures over to look for dates; her daughter's face in each picture told her everything she needed to know. Now she was determined to figure out how Catherine had handled her brief years as a cancer patient. Ella knew it was an exercise which was only causing her more pain, but she desperately had to know if her daughter had needed more from her. Knowing there was nothing she could change now, Ella still had to find her answer. Had she been the best mother she could have been to her daughter? If not, what had held her back?

One picture stood out as Ella looked over them this morning. It was a picture of Catherine and Anthony. The two rarely had their picture taken together, so Ella assumed one of the girls had taken charge of the camera. What struck Ella was the look of joy on her daughter's face as Anthony smiled at someone behind the camera. She was so happy to see that look on her sweet daughter's face, and she found herself grateful to Anthony for putting it there.

*

Sarah had grabbed the camera a few seconds before yelling, "Hey Daddy! I dare you to give Mom a big fat kiss!" Anthony smiled before turning to his lovely wife, and in that instant, Sarah took the picture. She knew it would be weeks before she would have the film developed, but she was certain she had captured a beautiful moment. Watching her parents kiss did not disgust her at all as it once had. Sarah was grateful to see her mom and dad enjoying each other. Her sixteenth birthday was only a couple of months away, and Sarah was aware of how sick her mom was looking. She found herself hoping her mom would be alive for her birthday. Sarah knew that would be the only gift to truly make it a sweet sixteen for her. Celebrating their birthdays together like they always had was the one gift she was not sure her mom could give her. Sarah slipped out of the room, not wanting her mom to see the tears that had sprung to her eyes.

Catherine was shocked when Sarah took the picture, but she was even more surprised when Anthony took his daughter's advice about the kiss. And what a kiss it was. She looked into his eyes and the years fell away. She saw the young serviceman she had fallen in love with so long ago. She felt like she could see their entire married life while staring into his eyes. They had so many happy memories together. She found it hard to look at him without thinking of the laughter they had shared almost every day. And all the good times traveling around the world together. The quiet moments they had spent together at home, as well as the rare times the two of them had snuck away for dinner and a movie. She thought of their long talks, and about how she had been the one whose shoulder he had cried on when his dad had unexpectedly died. Their marriage had been a good one, and she would not trade her time with him for anything.

But, as she thought about their life as a couple, she also thought about their three girls. She remembered the years when the girls were young. The days had been so hard, but they had disappeared quickly and her girls had grown up before her eyes. She had been everything to them. She remembered feeding them, bathing them, and comforting them as well as playing with them. She could tell they did not need her in the same way now, but she also knew a girl always would need her momma. Linda worried her most of all. She was just a baby, and a lot had been taken away from her. It pained

Catherine to watch her daughter's innocent childhood ripped away. She cringed as she thought of how helpless she was to help her little girl. This cancer was affecting all of them, and she had absolutely no power over it.

Anthony saw his wife's eyes cloud over, and reached out to hug her. "Hey, don't cry. You know how much I love you, right? You have always been my girl, and you always will be."

As he called her his girl, Catherine felt the tears course down her face. She loved him more than life itself, and would miss him so much. But she worried mostly about her girls. She had always been the one to take care of them. Would Anthony even know what to do? Who would Patricia and Sarah go to when they found boys they thought they loved? And Linda still needed a mommy who took care of her needs. Who would make sure she ate right? Who would remind her to dry her thick hair before heading out to get on the school bus? Catherine felt so helpless. It would be impossible to tell Anthony what he needed to know to do the job she had been doing with their children all these years. The role of mom was hers, and she was angry she was being forced to give it up. She wanted to be the one to do these things for her daughters, but she knew her time with them was short. How could she talk to Anthony about everything in her heart? She couldn't, so she didn't. She just wiped her tears, and looked up at him with a sad smile. "I love being your girl," was all she said. His smile told her she had made him happy, and wasn't that what she had always wanted? He didn't need to hear everything she was feeling.

*

Ella couldn't stop looking at the picture of her daughter with her young husband. They had been so in love. Her daughter looked impossibly happy. Ella wondered if their marriage had been the kind where they talked to each other about everything. She suspected not. Ella found herself talking to her daughter, even though she knew she could not hear her. "Oh, Catherine, did I fail you? I know you watched me and your daddy. Did you think being silent and invisible was the best way to be a wife? Honey, I'm just so so sorry."

Ella did not have the energy to put the pictures back in the box. She made her way to the bedroom, and climbed under the covers without even putting on her nightgown. She could not remember doing that since the day her daughter had died. In a way, she felt like she was reliving those final horrible days of her daughter's life. But, no matter how painful it was, she had to find her answers. It was the last thing she wanted to do before she found her way home to her sweet girl.

Chapter Thirteen

Ella woke up feeling different. She knew somehow she was close to the end. The end of this journey with the pictures, but also her end. She found herself looking forward to death. She wondered if Catherine had felt this way too. Had she been ready to give up the fight? Was there a point in her young life where death itself had seemed like a gift?

Ella knew today would be the day she would look at the final few pictures taken of her daughter. Today would be a challenge. Looking at these images would bring back some painful memories. Ella had spent years trying to get these thoughts out of her head. And now she was deliberately reliving the worst days of her life.

Shaking her head, she swung her legs over the bed and started her day.

The first picture was one of Catherine in the bed she had shared with Anthony. Ella looked at the blue striped sheets, and thought of how her daughter had always loved the color blue. She had always been so proud of her three girls, all with a different shade of blue eyes. Ella let her own eyes drift to the face of her daughter, and sucked in a deep breath. How close to the end her sweet baby girl had been in this picture. After all these years, Ella still could not quite understand why her daughter had to die.

*

Catherine really did not feel like smiling for the camera. She actually did not feel like smiling at all. She wanted to be alone, but she knew that was wrong. These days were not just hers; they belonged to her family too. So she smiled from her perch on the bed as Patricia took a quick picture before she slipped quietly out of the bedroom. Catherine had been lying in that bed all morning, listening to her family live life without her. It made her unbearably sad, knowing this would be their reality sooner than any of them knew. Hearing Linda as she woke up made Catherine sob into her pillow. Her youngest daughter still sounded like a happy little girl chattering away almost before her feet hit the floor. She listened to her youngest child call out that she wanted pancakes for breakfast. Catherine wished more than anything she could be the one to make them for her. She thought of the many hours she had stood over that stove flipping pancake after pancake for her family. She remembered the day she had instigated a pancake-eating contest, letting her girls stuff themselves in the name of fun. She was glad now for days like that. She was certain those memories would help keep her alive in the hearts of her girls. She had not realized the importance of what she was doing at the time, but she found herself grateful now for every moment, no matter how silly, she had spent with her children.

As she rested in bed, she let herself remember her life before cancer had invaded not only her body, but her entire world. She smiled a little as happy memories came to visit her. Every memory included her family. But every happy memory had to share space with the reality of her life coming to an end. Catherine felt the smile slide from her face as she held back a sob.

Listening to Patricia as she told Linda to come to the kitchen for breakfast, Catherine felt sad knowing this should have been her role. Knowing her oldest daughter was already cooking all the meals for the family made her even more aware that her girls were going to grow up without a mother. And she couldn't shake the feeling that her youngest would be the one to feel the loss in a much different way than the other two girls. But time was not on Catherine's side, and she knew there was no way to make a child as young as Linda able to understand the finality of death. Catherine felt overwhelmed with hopelessness as she thought about her little girl growing up without a mother. Who would take care of her baby? So she fought death, hanging on to the hope that if she lived long enough Linda might understand why she had to die.

Later, Catherine heard Anthony tell Patricia and Sarah to take Linda with them to the store. He said he wanted the house to be quiet for a few hours so their mom could rest. She wanted to shout out to him that she wanted to hear them. She needed to hear them. She needed to carry their voices with her. Catherine knew it would not be long now, and she wanted as much time as she could get with her family. But she knew everything Anthony did was out of his love for her. She still could not believe the love they had shared all these years. She only wished they could grow old together as they had planned. It all seemed like a nightmare to her, one she knew she could not wake up from no matter how hard she tried. So she let her children go.

As Catherine drifted off to sleep, she thought about the camera Patricia had been holding earlier that morning. It held what would probably be the last roll of film with pictures of her on it. At what point would her oldest daughter drive to the store and drop it off? Would she worry the pictures would not turn out right, knowing this film contained her final link to her mother? It made Catherine's heart ache knowing Patricia would soon be going through this without her. She wondered if she had been the only one who had noticed the way her precious firstborn had been taking more pictures lately. Patricia was trying desperately to hold onto her mom, but she just did not know how. It made Catherine sad to know her daughter, who would be turning eighteen soon, had such a heavy burden on her. She had watched Patricia grow up a lot these past three years, and she was proud of her and the strength she was showing. Catherine knew her daughter would need that strength as she took on her new role of mother to her sisters. She knew her firstborn was ready for the cooking and the cleaning, but she also knew the other burdens she was about to bear would rob her of her last teen years. She knew her daughter would be forced to grow up in a way she shouldn't have to. Catherine felt a familiar pang of guilt, and wished once again for the chance to continue being a mother to her precious children.

She then thought about Sarah, who would turn sixteen just a day after her own birthday. A birthday she herself hoped she would see. She would be turning 38, but she knew in her heart she would never live to see 39. Even to her, it seemed an impossibly young age to die. Her sweet daughter deserved a party for her sixteenth birthday like the one they had thrown for Patricia just two short years ago. But Catherine barely had enough strength to walk from her bed to the bathroom. There would be no party. She would never make another birthday cake. And she knew in her heart she had bought the last birthday present she would ever buy. Her gift to Sarah would be living long enough to wish her a happy birthday. She also sadly realized her death would most likely happen close to her daughter's birthday. She felt tears roll down her face thinking her daughter would always suffer on her birthday because of her.

And Linda, who was just twelve, would not know what had happened when her mommy breathed her final breath. Linda made Catherine cry the hardest, the tears turning into sobs now. She had noticed the way Anthony was gently pulling her youngest daughter away from her. She knew he was doing it to make it easier on their baby girl when she no longer had a mommy to hug or cuddle up to. It tore a piece of her heart out every time he kept Linda from her. Part of Catherine wanted to keep her baby home from school with her, letting her snuggle in bed with her all day. But she knew this was selfish. She could only hope Linda would one day realize the depth of her love for her.

Thinking about her girls growing up without her was too much to take in, so Catherine carefully rolled over onto her side and let herself fall asleep, knowing she would dream, as always, of them. They were her babies, and she hoped her dreams would be filled with happier times of the four of them together. She wished for her daughters to all three always have the same kind of happy dreams about her.

*

Ella held that picture in her hands for a long time. She saw the sad look in her daughter's tired eyes. She wondered who had taken the picture, making her daughter put on such a brave smile. She knew this had been one of the final days of her sweet daughter's life. She remembered exactly how Catherine had looked right before she had left her home for the last time, heading to the hospital where she would drift away forever. She would always be grateful she had been staying with them that night when the ambulance had been called. She still could not believe her daughter had been strong enough to pick up the phone and call for the ambulance herself, knowing leaving her bed meant never returning. Watching those men put her daughter on that gurney and take her from her home had almost made Ella fall to her knees. The look on Linda's face as she slowly opened her bedroom door and peeked out to see what was going on in the hall had given Ella the strength to go on. She remembered going to her granddaughter to explain how her mommy was going to the hospital. Linda was the only one in the house who did not seem to understand that Catherine would never come back.

Ella remembered how her brave daughter had clung to life for three more weeks after being taken away in that ambulance. At the end of the first week in the hospital, they all gathered around her bed to quietly celebrate Patricia's 18th birthday. Catherine had asked her mother to please buy a birthday card so she could sign one last wish to her daughter. In her shaky hand, she managed to simply write, "I love you. Mom." even though she had so much more she wanted to say to her first child. The day before her own birthday, Catherine's two oldest girls had tapped on her hospital window as they held up the family dog for their mom to see. Precious had been a member of the family for many years, and it made Catherine smile weakly from her pillow as she saw her dog for what would be the last time. Catherine was barely holding onto life on her own birthday. Her family stood around the bed, but there were no presents or any of the other trappings of a birthday party. The nurses stopped in frequently to give their mom more morphine, and the girls did their best to keep sadness off of their faces. The next day was Sarah's Sweet Sixteen. Catherine was barely holding on by then, but managed to give her daughter's hand a weak squeeze as she smiled up at her from a sweat-drenched pillow. That would be the last time any of them would see their mom's beautiful eyes open. The next day she slipped in a coma. Even then she fought death for four more days, finally drifting away peacefully early one morning before the family came to visit her for the day.

Looking at the picture and remembering her daughter's final days, Ella wondered if Catherine had known how close she was to the end when she was smiling at the camera. Deep in her heart, she suspected her daughter had known. Ella tried to remember the last time they had spoken, but the years were not being kind to her tonight, and she found it hard to remember.

Chapter Fourteen

She could not do this anymore. Ella wondered around the yard late in the morning, knowing what she was really avoiding was the box of pictures and the memories they dredged up for her. She wondered not for the first time why she had ever started this project. She would, most likely, be dead soon too. Her family could swoop in, and divide up her meager belongings. None of them would ever need to know how these pictures had haunted her. She wondered if she was the only one who knew the truth about how the pictures had been saved. She remembered going to see her granddaughters a few weeks after her daughter had died. Frank had dropped her off, telling her to ask Anthony to bring her home later that evening. She had spent the day cooking and freezing meals while the girls sat in the kitchen with her, talking to her about everything she was sure they would rather be telling their own mother. Later, when Anthony drove her home, she summoned up enough courage to ask him how he was doing.

*

"How are you really doing? Anthony, you can talk to me. I know you are hurting as much as Frank and me. Maybe even more so. Please talk to me."

But instead of answering her, he simply pulled something from his front pocket and placed it in her hand. Looking down, she saw that he had handed her a book of matches. Not knowing what this could possibly mean, Ella just looked at her son-in-law. Something told her to just be quiet until he wanted to tell her what it was all about.

"Ella, maybe you could keep those for me? They have been in the pocket of my pants since the day I had to bury her. I can't tell you how many times I've almost burned down the entire house, just needing to escape her memory." Crying now, he continued, "It's just that she's everywhere, in every room. I can't escape the memories. Don't get me wrong. I love her more than life itself. It's just that I know I'm supposed to be strong for our girls even when I can barely make myself get out of bed in the mornings. I know that's what Catherine wanted me to do. But I just can't help how I feel. I don't know how to go on without her."

Ella sat in silence until Anthony turned his car into her driveway. She finally spoke. "Anthony, go home and find that poem she wrote for you. One thing I know is my daughter loved you and those girls more than she loved her own life." Reaching over to hug him before she got out of the car, Ella took the time to say a silent prayer for him. She knew he had lost part of his heart too.

*

Thinking about the pictures and how they had almost been lost to her, Ella decided she needed to finish her project. Besides, she had grown tired, as she knew she would, so she made her way back inside the house. As the screen door slammed behind her, she went to the kitchen sink and filled a glass with water. After drinking as much as she could, she decided to rest on the couch. But when she got to the couch, she saw the pictures she had not put away the night before.

Deciding she owed this much and more to her daughter, Ella allowed the pictures to take her to the past again. She truly did want to understand what her daughter was feeling during this time in her life. But today Ella found herself also wanting to simply revisit her times with her daughter. She wanted to relive every trip to the grocery store together, every time they took the girls shopping for school clothes in the late summer, and every time she had visited her daughter to comfort her after a trip to the hospital. She wanted to hear their laughter as they watched the three girls who meant the world to both of them. She wanted to remember the easy times she had once taken for granted. She wanted to think of happy times, when things were as they should be, when they didn't realize they had nothing to worry about. She wanted to remember times when they had been blissfully unaware of the nightmare to come. But Ella knew she had to look at all the pictures, and they did not all make her remember happier times.

Ella picked up a picture which showed Catherine sitting outside. She could tell by the scarf on her daughter's head, and by the way her clothes seemed to fall off of her body, that this had been taken days before she went to the hospital for the final time. This picture made Ella cry. The tears flowed heavily, and Ella had to set the picture aside while she got herself under control. This picture clearly showed how cancer had destroyed Catherine's body, stealing her life away little by little. In this picture, her daughter had been maybe a month or two away from her 38th birthday, which had always seemed impossibly young to Ella. How had her little girl died at such a young age? It still didn't seem real to her. She didn't think it ever would.

She looked deeply into the eyes of her daughter, and saw a strength she hadn't seen in some of the other pictures. A quiet strength that made Ella proud of her youngest child. Ella knew at that moment that Catherine had known she was about to die. She realized her daughter must have been in agonizing pain, knowing she was leaving her husband and three young daughters behind. It must have been horrible and so very scary for her, but the picture showed none of that. It showed a young mother who was determined to make her final days matter to her family. It was a picture of a woman who was putting the needs of others above her own. There was not an ounce of selfish pity in her daughter's eyes. Ella was prouder of her daughter as she looked at that picture than she ever had been. She knew she had missed many opportunities to tell her daughter how much she loved her, and that she was proud of her, but she also knew the only way to go back in time was through these pictures.

As Ella intently studied her daughter in the faded photograph, she realized for the first time where her daughter's silent invisible strength had come from. She felt like she was seeing herself, not her daughter, as she looked at the picture. With sudden clarity, Ella realized the silence that had plagued her throughout her life had been the most important example she had given her daughter to follow. She realized now that Catherine had learned the gift of silent strength from watching her all those years. Ella now knew she had given her daughter the gift that had sustained her during her final days. Ella wept almost uncontrollably as she realized the quiet invisible way she had lived her own life had been seen by her daughter. She understood for the first time that she had been the one who had gotten her daughter through her final days. She had not been there in the way a lot of mothers would have been, and Catherine had not asked for her help the way some daughters would have, but somehow their love over the years had created something that had made her daughter strong enough to die. She knew now that her example of how to live had been the one thing that had helped her daughter at the end of her life.

Ella finally realized she could put away the box of photos. She had found at last what she needed to leave this world. She finally felt peace. She decided she would give these pictures to Catherine's daughters. It would be what Catherine would have wanted; it would be Ella's final gift to her daughter. It would be the gift Catherine herself could have never given to them, as much as she may have wanted to. Ella would gladly do this and so much more for her daughter. The time had passed for helping her daughter in practical ways. She no longer had the luxury of picking up the phone just to let her daughter hear the voice of love that truly is unique to mothers. But, even though she no longer had the chance to do the many things for her daughter she wished she could do, she could do this one thing. She could help Catherine's daughters find the peace she suspected had eluded them all these years too.

Ella smiled as she got into bed that night. She felt lighter than air. Her work was complete, and she knew hers had been a life well-lived. A hard life, full of intense pain, but a good life just the same. She was pleased, as she fell asleep, with her job as a mother. She knew it was the role she had always been meant to play, and she finally had the assurance she had played it well.

Chapter Fifteen

Ella was still tired when she got out of bed the next day. Her body felt stiff, and it was a real effort to even move. She thought this was strange even though she had been more tired than usual lately, but at her age she really did not know what was normal anymore. She decided to skip breakfast, and went straight to the pictures. Shuffling out of her bedroom, she felt her muscles loosening up just a bit. She laughed softly as she imagined Frank seeing her now. Would he even recognize the old woman she had somehow turned into? After finding a comfortable spot on the couch, Ella looked at the pictures. With determination she set to work. She was surprised how quickly she was able to divide the photos into three neat piles. Moving the photos from their spot on her couch, Ella headed to the adjacent dining room. Stacking them on the dining room table, the same table where Catherine had eaten as a young girl and then as a young mother, Ella felt the memories well up inside of her. She smiled as she realized the memories brought nothing but happiness this morning. She knew her daughter would be pleased with this project.

Patricia's stack contained each picture of her as a baby, and also the ones that showed her mother's strength. Ella knew that Patricia, as the oldest, had seen how strong her momma was at the end. She wanted her to have those memories. Patricia was a capable woman in her own right, but Ella also knew she carried a burden around every day, never knowing if she had been there enough for her mom. Patricia had been a mature teenager, and was now a woman who would have made her mother proud. She had a soft side under all that strength, just like her mother had. In many ways, Patricia, of all three girls, was the most like Catherine. But she had been little more than a child when her mother had gotten sick. Ella hoped these pictures would finally let Patricia accept the fact that, as a young teenager, it had never been her responsibility to make her mother well. She could only hope the pictures would be enough to finally give Patricia the peace she so desperately needed.

Sarah's stack included pictures of her mom's playful side. There was the stack of pictures tied with the yellow ribbon that contained all of the pictures of Sarah as a baby. But Ella also wanted Sarah to remember how happy her mom had been. Being barely a teenager when her mother had gotten sick had affected Sarah in so many ways. Ella knew Sarah, to this day, worried that her typical teenage antics had been hard on her mother. Seeing these pictures of her mom smiling and happy would, hopefully, help Sarah understand that, as her mother's second child, Catherine had expected everything Sarah had thrown at her. These pictures clearly showed the love between Catherine and Sarah, and Ella's hope was for Sarah to finally forgive herself. She knew all about guilt, and she was sure her daughter had as well. If she could free her granddaughter of any lingering effects of teenage guilt, she knew Catherine would have been grateful.

Linda's little stack of baby pictures was next. Ella decided to include all the pictures of Catherine looking at the camera the way she always looked at Linda. Ella knew not to include any pictures of when her daughter had been at her sickest and lowest points. Linda needed to see happier times of her mom, and Ella picked the pictures that showed Catherine looking like the happy young mother she had been. Ella knew that, unlike the two older girls, Linda had only known one side of her mom. She was not old enough to ever see her mom as the wonderful person she was; she just knew her as her mommy. Ella wanted Linda to see the strong, capable woman her daughter had been. Most importantly, Ella desperately wanted to erase every memory from Linda's mind of those horrifying final weeks of Catherine's illness. Somehow, Ella knew this was a gift Catherine would have given to Linda if she had been able to. Doing this would have made her daughter happy, and Ella had only ever wanted her sweet girl to be pleased.

Her job was finally done. Ella decided just to leave the pictures on the table. It wasn't like she used it for anything else these days.

She could not remember the last time she had eaten at that table, preferring to sit in the small kitchen for her daily meals. The smaller room somehow made it seem less obvious that she was alone, eating a meal she had prepared with no thought of leftovers. And she had grown used to eating in silence over the years.

Ella walked around the house later that day, letting the memories of her long life flow over her. She could almost hear the sound of her three boys, the house always so loud with yells and taunts mixed with laughter. She remembered the new sound of a little girl in the house. It had been so different when Catherine had been born. The house was quieter with her in it somehow even though their family had grown larger. The boys had calmed down after their sister had been born. And Catherine had filled their house with the soft, sweet sounds of a girl. If she listened closely enough she could hear Joe telling Jimmy and Timothy to go get Catherine so she could play with them. She had such good memories of her four children playing together, with Catherine always at the center of it all. Ella laughed and cried as she remembered both good times and bad. And she found herself incredibly tired.

Deciding to take an early nap, Ella did something she had never done before. Even though she got on her knees every night of her life to pray, she had never once prayed before a nap. Today felt different, so she lowered herself to her knees before climbing into bed. She needed this nap to get ready for tomorrow. She had called her three granddaughters earlier to ask them to come for a visit the next day. She had listened with delight as each girl had excitedly shared the kind of news unique to young women with her. She loved them more than they would ever know. She would give them the world if she could, just like she knew they would do anything for her. Catherine had done an amazing job as a mother, and she intended to tell each girl that very thing when she saw them tomorrow. She couldn't wait to see the looks on their faces as she handed them each their stack of pictures. She knew they would laugh and cry like she had, but she also knew they would want to talk about their mother. And she was finally ready to have that talk.

Becoming Invisible